I0693136

THE SLAVE OF APOLLO

First Edition

Published by The Nazca Plains Corporation
Las Vegas, Nevada
2011

ISBN: 978-1-61098-288-7
E-book: 978-1-61098-289-4

Published by

The Nazca Plains Corporation ®
4640 Paradise Rd, Suite 141
Las Vegas NV 89109-8000

PUBLISHER'S NOTE
The Slave of Apollo is a work of fiction created wholly by Lew
Bull's imagination. All characters are fictional and any resemblance
to any persons living or deceased is purely by accident. No portion
of this book reflects any real person or events.

Cover Photos,
Robert Lerich and Andrei Vishnyakov

Art Director,
Blake Stephens

THE SLAVE OF APOLLO

First Edition

LEW BULL

DEDICATION

Rob – Thank you for your great friendship and for
being such a very caring person. May you always
enjoy happiness in your music and your travels.

CONTENTS

CHAPTER 1

THE ARRIVAL

Holidays have always been an important part of my life, along with sex and having fun, but deciding where to spend a holiday had also proved problematic for me. I enjoyed traveling to other parts of the world, and making the decision as to where to go often created turmoil in my life. Each time I picked up a travel brochure, I found a new place to visit, so planning my summer vacation was going to be no different from in past years.

Each time I was due to take a holiday I would visit my local travel agency, bring home a bundle of brochures to ponder over, pour myself a drink and settle down to at least two days of browsing.

However, as it was the start of summer, I decided this particular year to approach my best friends, Brad and Clint for their advice and guidance on where to spend the summer vacation. It was also natural that I invite them to come along with me for the vacation as we had been friends for approximately a year after I had met them in strange circumstances. I say 'strange', but for many people, their meeting might not be construed as being strange.

One evening I had gone to a massage parlor. I had been feeling in need of a pampering massage, and perhaps a little extra thrown in, so I took myself off to a massage parlor that I had seen advertised in the local newspaper. Although this was not my usual habit, I had decided that it was worth a try and so set off. At the massage parlor, which was a large house with a number of different rooms, I was ushered into a lounge area, offered a drink and told that I could meet the different masseurs who were on duty that night. After having been introduced to the various young men who were available, and what a difficult choice that was, I had chosen Brad because I liked his looks and he seemed the most genuine of the guys shown to me. When I say 'genuine' I meant he was my ideal – down to earth, straight-forward without airs and graces, and pretty easy to talk to. However, unbeknown to me, when he had entered the darkened bedroom to commence the massage, his best friend, Clint, who had not been introduced to me, had also slipped into the room.

Brad stripped off to reveal his beautifully buffed body and the two of us readied ourselves for the massage. Brad had a fine body and an even finer appendage hanging between his legs. I stripped and lay on my stomach on the bed – the reason for this was obvious – I was getting the start of a hard on. Brad had started to massage my back and very soon when I had turned over onto my stomach, I saw that both he and I had erections that competed equally with each other. Brad proceeded to massage between my legs and in the area of my ass, balls and cock. This made both my erection and his even harder. He then let his hands glide over my nipples, grazing them gently as he did so and traveling down my chest until he slid down the length of my body and took my erect cock deep into his throat. Oh the feeling was orgasmic and …! I could go into details here, but we might never get to the real reason for me mentioning their names. One thing led to another and eventually, after some time of Brad and I pleasuring each other, Clint, who had been surreptitiously hiding and watching us, came out of his 'hiding place' to join us in our fun and that's how the three of us first became acquainted. After that exciting experience, where both Clint and Brad had the pleasure of sliding their massive cocks into me, I often went back to the massage parlor, but always insisted that I have both Brad and Clint giving me a massage. You know, there's nothing more exhilarating and sensual than a four-hand massage, especially if other parts of the human body are also brought into play! Try it sometime!

Although they were both very good looking young men, Brad, who was twenty-six years of age, had, in my opinion, a far more defined body than Clint, but Clint's physique was more of a body-builder's and therefore more bulky, yet not unattractive. Physically, they were both drop-dead gorgeous. Clint was two years older than Brad and I was the eldest of the three of us, being thirty. I got on very well with both of them, but I did find that on occasions, Clint often tended to be a little moody, so when we decided to go away together for a holiday, Brad and I joked with Clint and said that unless he promised not to be moody on the holiday, he could not come with us.

Clint was a serious young man and I don't think he trusted Brad and me on our own in a foreign place, so he insisted on coming with us to keep an eye on our behavior, so he said. Brad, on the other hand, was a happy-go-lucky sort of guy who was fun to be with, but that does not mean that Clint wasn't fun to be with, it's just that Brad seemed to have a similar temperament to mine.

After poring over dozens of travel brochures, looking at islands and cities, cruises and backpacking trips through jungles, beaches and mountain holidays, the foreign place that we all decided to visit was Greece and its islands. Looking at the magnificent photos in the brochures convinced us that this was the ideal place where we could relax and generally chill out, away from the busy, frenzied city life. We admired the beautiful pictures of azure seas, pristine white buildings and marveled the fact that the beaches were beautiful and exciting: nudity being allowed on some of them! I had visited Greece once before, but as neither of the other guys had ever been there; Brad bought himself a travel guide on Greece, in order to read up something of the places and the way of life. Of course, we had all known a Greek man or two in our time, but as I explained to Brad and Clint, Greeks from Greece are not the same as the ones back home.

"What do you mean?" asked Brad.

"Well, to start with, the real Greeks are more good looking and they're not pushy," I replied.

"What do you mean by real Greeks? Don't you think the Greeks living here are real?" queried Clint.

"No, what I mean is Greeks who live in Greece, not Americanized Greeks."

"And in what way are they not pushy?" questioned Clint.

"From a business perspective; for example, when you go into a taverna and order something to eat or drink, they don't want your money straight away, they want you to relax and enjoy yourself; get to know you, in a way. In other words, I think they're good businessmen, because they encourage you to stay longer and spend more money. They make your stay with them relaxing and stress-free, and you get more time to get to know them – if you know what I mean!"

"That sounds like my sort of life-style," added Brad. "And the men?"

"That was what I was talking about – getting to know them, but wait and see," I replied.

"Are they as good-looking as the Greeks back home?" continued Brad.

"You'll see for yourself," I replied.

"You know there are times when I could strangle you," joked Brad, getting frustrated by my non-committal answers. "If I think of George Michael, the singer – he's Greek and I think he's hunky," continued Brad.

"Oh well, he's the exception, and he's not American," I replied, agreeing that George Michael was good looking.

I could sense that Brad was eager to get to Greece, if not for the beaches and beauty, at least for the men, but I think Clint was a little worried about his friend's desperate need to get his hands on a Greek.

"I'm a little worried about you two," quipped Clint, nonchalantly, "such concerns for Greek men when we've got each other."

"Sure," replied Brad, "but variety is the spice of life."

"In any case, that's why you go on holiday – to meet other men," I answered.

Once having gone through all the brochures and Brad's travel guide, by mutual agreement, we decided that we were going to fly to Athens, spend a few days there seeing the historical sites and then go off to the island of Mykonos for a while. Mykonos was the most obvious choice as we'd all heard stories about the exciting night-life to be had on the island, and that is what we wanted – fun! Obviously, while we were based on Mykonos, I had explained to the guys that we would be able to visit other islands in the surrounding area, by taking ferries, or we could merely stay on Mykonos and enjoy what it had to offer. Brad had read up on Mykonos, and with great delight informed us of the beach potential there was on the island.

"We have to go to Super Paradise," he said excitedly with his eyes lighting up.

"Why, what's so special about Super Paradise," retorted Clint, with an almost bored voice.

"Naked bodies!" exclaimed Brad rubbing his hands together with glee and licking his lips.

"There you go again! The way you're going on," continued a tired-sounding Clint, "anyone would think that you'd never seen a naked body. Tell me, when you massage, do you do it with the client's clothes on?"

"No," answered Brad.

"So what's so important about seeing naked bodies when you see them every day?" continued Clint.

"Well, not so many all at the same time out in the open, or with great tans and I'm sure, with fabulous bodies," replied Brad.

"Come on, you two. Control your hormones," I said, trying to prevent this discussion leading to an unnecessary argument and potentially derailing our holiday to Greece.

In the days that followed, there was much excitement and activities as we prepared for our holiday. Appropriate clothes had to be purchased; sun tan lotion was needed to prevent us becoming lobster-looking and generally our over-all appearance needed to be enhanced, so Clint and Brad spent a few extra days at the gym. I realized that both Brad and Clint, as well as myself, to a large extent, were going on this holiday to have a good time, but I was also interested in the cultural side of Greece, having studied a course in Greek civilization while at university, training to become a teacher.

At last, the day of our departure arrived and we set off on our flight to Athens. We boarded the Olympic Airways plane and found our seats. A sense of excitement began to develop and soon we were chatting excitedly about what we were planning to do when we got there. Once we had taken off, Clint began complaining about the flight stewards not being attractive.

"If this is what the Greek men look like," he complained, "then I think we've made a bad choice."

"Have a drink, Clint. In fact, have a couple of drinks, because the more you drink the better looking the guys become," I suggested, as both Brad and I laughed.

But still as the flight continued, so Clint continued to complain. Brad and I tried to ignore his comments and simply told him to wait until we arrived in Greece, then he could make a judgment. This tended to keep him quiet for a while and the three of us just tried our best to relax and enjoy the flight.

During the flight, I noticed that Brad became interested in one of the flight stewards and kept hopping up and down in his seat, under the pretext that he wanted something to drink or needed to go to the toilet. This continued for many hours until Clint spoke up.

"Are you cruising that guy, Brad?"

"I don't know what you're talking about," came the retort.

"Why don't you find a secluded spot somewhere on the plane and sort the guy out," replied a tired Clint.

I merely smiled, knowing that if Brad was that determined to do something with the guy, he'd manage somehow.

Both Clint and I managed to doze off to sleep but Brad continued to make advances to the flight attendant.

Early the following morning, our plane landed in a hot, sultry Athens.

"Did you score last night?" I asked, surreptitiously as we began to disembark.

Brad returned a glowing face to me and grinned.

"I take it that means yes?"

He nodded and grinned even more broadly.

"Where?" I whispered.

"Toilet at the back of the plane. I had to join the Mile-High Club."

"You're such a slut!"

I giggled at the thought, but Clint didn't notice either of us talking quietly to each other.

We went through customs without any problems and fought our way through the babbling, expressive Greeks in the foyer of the terminal building until we found our contact that was going to drive us to our hotel in the center of Athens.

A short little man, who looked about in his late thirties, bearing a placard with our names on was standing near the doorway to the exit. We noticed the placard before we noticed him and made our way towards him. We introduced ourselves and he told us his name was Dimitri and that if we needed anything while we were in Athens, he was the guy to contact. He seemed a very innocuous and inconspicuous type of character, yet friendly and willing to help. He had the typical olive-colored skin of most Mediterranean people, was clean-shaven and had short dark hair. We climbed into his rather battered car, which looked like it had been in many an accident, and sped off towards the center of the city.

Poor Brad was sitting in the front of the car next to Dimitri, and at times I thought Brad was going to faint, because of the way that Dimitri was driving; we seemed to be flying through the traffic, dodging cars and motorcycles at a death-defying speed. It was a wonder that no one was killed or injured. Maybe this was why Dimitri's car was so battered, from bumping other vehicles.

However, Dimitri did try to make our journey into the center of the city enjoyable by pointing out landmarks and historical buildings to us, like an inevitable tourist guide. Eventually, having wound through some very narrow streets, we arrived at our small hotel situated in the Plaka area. The car came to a sudden halt as though we had collided into something. We all breathed a sigh of relief when Dimitri told us we were at the hotel.

Dimitri unloaded our bags and carried them into the hotel foyer for us. He spoke to the receptionist and then hovered around us while we booked into the hotel. Once we had been allocated our room, which we were going to share, Dimitri insisted on picking up our bags and proceeded to take us to our room, as though he were the bellboy employed by the hotel. We weren't quite sure why he was doing it, but we decided to let him do his thing, so to speak. When we arrived at our room, he put the key into the lock and opened the door for us. We entered into a clean, simply furnished room with two single beds and a bathroom and toilet off the room. Dimitri placed our bags on the floor and then looked at the beds. I was not sure what was going through his mind, but he then pointed to the beds, looked back at us and said, "Two beds, three people."

"Yes," I replied.

"How three people sleep with two beds?" he asked in his broken English.

Clint muttered under his breath, "Use your imagination!"

"We push the beds together to make one big bed then we can sleep," I said, smiling at the little man. "I think that will be all," I continued, "if we need anything we'll call you, but I think at the moment, all we want to do is have a shower and some rest."

"Thanks Dimitri," said Brad opening the bedroom door, in an effort to usher him out. At last, Dimitri, looking a little dejected, got the message and left us to unpack and relax.

"Were we supposed to tip him?" asked Clint when Dimitri had departed.

"I don't know," I replied. "I know the cost of the transfer was included in our initial booking, but carrying suitcases – that's something different."

Even though we were indoors, the oppressive heat from outside still managed to get through to us. We each had a shower to freshen up, got changed into shorts and T-shirts, because of the intense heat, and unpacked. We then threw ourselves onto the single beds that had been pushed together and fell asleep. We didn't sleep long, maybe an hour or so, but after we had rested, we went downstairs to start looking around Athens.

As we exited from the hotel foyer, we heard, amongst a cacophony of other noises, a loud hooter blaring from a car nearby. We all turned in the same direction to see Dimitri waving frantically at us. He had obviously left us in our room and come downstairs to wait for us. We waved back as we didn't have the heart to ignore him, in fact it was almost impossible to ignore him, he was becoming like a leech, so after a quick discussion, we moved over to where his car was parked.

"You ready to see my city," he said excitedly, wiping perspiration from his brow.

"Yes," said Brad, almost resignedly, "but I'm not sitting in the front this time."

I could see the expression on both Brad's and Clint's faces, so I offered a possible solution.

"OK, I'll take my life in my hands," I said opening the front door and sliding in next to Dimitri while the other two clambered into the back of the car, and off we went.

We wound our way through narrow streets, packed with cars and people, busily going about their daily business. Again, we sped through the streets as though we were driving to an emergency, each of us clasping onto anything that would hopefully protect us in the event that we crashed.

The first place that Dimitri wanted to show us was the Acropolis, which I suppose all tourists have to see. The sight from the top was amazing and as this was Brad and Clint's first visit, I think they were suitably impressed with what they saw, both from a historical point of view as well as an aesthetic one. The city of Athens sprawled out below us and the sight made me wonder what it would have been like living in the times of the ancient Greeks. Admittedly there wouldn't have been cars and chaos as we had experienced, but I was sure there would still have been a feeling of busy activities that still pervaded the modern city. Once we had wandered around the ruins, getting a historical account from Dimitri, and admired the view, he told us it was time to head off to our next port of call.

Back in the coolness of the car with its air-conditioning, we headed off to visit the original Olympic stadium. All the time, Dimitri was very animated in his descriptions of the things that we passed, and every now and then I noticed that during his animated conversation, his left hand would land, either accidentally or not I don't know, on my right leg and remain there while he spoke. Out of the corner of my eye I could see Brad grinning from ear to ear every time this happened. This continued for the duration of the morning while Dimitri gave us a guided tour of Athens and constantly kept Clint and Brad amused in the back seat.

At length, we returned to our hotel around lunchtime. Out of decency, we invited Dimitri to have lunch with us as he had refused any money for taking us on the tour. It was actually great having him there because he was able to speak the language and could explain to us what various things were that were on the menu. After a lengthy lunch, where Dimitri continued to regale us with stories of his wonderful city, we decided that all we wanted to do was go upstairs to our room and have a sleep, in readiness for the evening. After lunch we excused ourselves from Dimitri and made our way up to our room, where the three of us fell onto the two beds and went to sleep, exhausted both from the intense heat and the jet lag.

At about seven in the evening I woke to hear someone having a shower. I looked across the bed and saw Clint lying there, so I knew that it was Brad having a shower. I rose from the bed and went to the window. The sun was still beating down and one could still feel the heat coming up from the streets below. This is one of the beauties of Greece, particularly on the islands, that the sun sets late in summer so your hours of swimming and sunbathing are very long.

My body felt clammy from the heat and humidity, so I also had another shower after Brad had finished his, and got dressed for the evening. Once dressed, the three of us went downstairs and out into the heat.

"I don't believe it," I said, nudging Brad.

"What?" he replied?

"Look across the street."

Both Clint and Brad looked, and there was Dimitri, sitting in his car. I wondered if he had spent the entire afternoon there waiting for us.

"He's becoming a nuisance," said Clint rather irritably.

"I told you Greeks were friendly," I laughed.

"That's not being friendly," remonstrated Clint, "that's being a pest."

"So, what are we going to do?" asked Brad. "Do we sneak off without him seeing us, or do we go with him?"

Having spent the morning with him, he was beginning to grow on us. Although he was not very attractive, he had a rugged, weather-beaten look about him and he had a pleasant personality that was quite endearing.

"Come on, guys, at least he knows the place and he can show us around," I said. I'm not sure if it was what I had said, or whether it was the heat coming from the streets, but they both agreed with me and we crossed the road to Dimitri's car with its air-conditioning. He was so pleased to see us, he said, "Now I treat you."

"But you've already treated us today," I replied.

"No, I treat you special tonight."

We told Clint that it was his turn to sit in the front and Brad and I clambered into the back of the car, and off we set.

As we drove through the city, Brad and I noticed that Dimitri never touched Clint's leg like he had touched mine, and I also noticed how often, when he was chatting to us, he kept looking at me in the rear-view mirror and smiling. This man was flirting with me, but I didn't worry unduly.

We spent a wonderful evening having dinner, where there was a display of Greek dancing with the inevitable breaking of plates, so characteristic of Greek culture, and then we had some drinks at a bar and heard about the history of the city. I noticed, as we sat in the bar having drinks, how often Dimitri's leg kept rubbing up against mine. I wasn't quite sure what to do because I didn't know what the other two had planned for that night, nor was I sure how they'd react if I told them about Dimitri's flirting with me. Eventually, after a very pleasant evening of drinking, eating and breaking plates a la Greek style, Dimitri took us back to our hotel. We thanked him for a wonderful day and went up to our room where we all decided we needed another shower to cool down from the heat of the evening. We all showered again and then we all lay naked on the beds in the dark of the room with Clint and Brad taking up most of the one bed, while I occupied the other. We were lying there talking about what we had done and seen that day, when there was a faint knock at the door.

"Who on earth can that be?" asked Brad. "Well I'm not getting up," he continued.

We all lay there, no one moving. Again the knock came, this time a little louder.

"All right, I'll get it," I said, getting up from the bed and crossing over to the door.

The only light coming into the room at that moment was from the moonlight streaming in through the open window. I opened the door a little and the passage light revealed Dimitri standing there. I opened the door wider and stared at him; his eyes followed up and down my naked body.

"Dimitri, what are you doing here?" I enquired. I heard movement on the bed.

"I have come back to see you because I promised you a special night," he said.

"It's a bit late and we have to get up early in the morning to go off to the islands," I replied knowing how annoyed Clint would be if I invited him into our room to chat.

This, however, didn't seem to put him off. He stood in the brightly lit corridor; his eyes transfixed on my naked body, and suddenly rubbed his hand across his crotch. I could see that he had the beginnings of an erection, which was showing through his weathered trousers. I could also see that he was not keen on leaving so I eventually said, "I suppose you'd better come in before somebody else sees me naked."

Clint and Brad had by this time huddled closer together on the one bed and pretended to be asleep but I knew all the time they were wide-awake and probably laughing inside or becoming irritated by this man. I moved back to my bed and lay down. Dimitri took off his shirt to reveal a stocky, yet well-defined body, which I could see in the moonlight. He then lowered his trousers to reveal a well-hung, uncut cock that was in the process of becoming even harder. He slipped onto the bed next to me and wrapped his arms around me. At no time did he try to kiss me, perhaps because it would have appeared unmanly to him, but he was determined as to what he wanted to do – give me pleasure, as well as himself. I felt him take hold of my head and push it down towards his stomach. I could smell the sweaty odor coming from his body as he embraced my head in his muscular arms.

I could feel his hardened cock pressing up against my chest and soon my own hard-on was rubbing against his legs. I decided to please him so I moved lower towards his cock. I took it into my mouth and ran my tongue over it, feeling his hood slide back to uncover his glans. He groaned gently and I heard what sounded like a snigger come from either Brad or Clint. My mouth continued to slide along his lengthy cock for some time and then I felt him pull my head up towards his. He turned me onto my left side so that my back was to him and I was pushed up against Brad and Clint. I heard the tearing of foil and felt him putting a condom onto his erect cock and then felt it nudge my asshole. Slowly and painlessly his hard cock entered me and he began a series of short, sharp stabbing movements. Once he got going, both beds began to squeak and move. I wondered what Brad and Clint were thinking – in fact with all this movement, they might be at it as well, I thought. His thrusts were like that of a frantic man, one who was in a hurry to finish what he was doing. With each thrust, I was pushed up against Brad, who could obviously feel my hard-on rubbing against him. I could feel Dimitri's movement become more frantic and his breathing become heavier until he exploded in me with a groaning sound that seemed to go on forever. Finally I felt him relax and slowly withdraw from me. He gave me a quick squeeze and slid off the bed. I saw him dress without speaking and leave the room. The whole act couldn't have lasted more than five minutes. Brad turned to me and said, "That was strange! Didn't he even say goodbye?"

All three of us burst out laughing after he had departed, but I lay there not quite knowing what to think. It hadn't been special for me, but I hoped that it had been special for Dimitri in some way or another. I then put my arms around Brad and Clint, my still erect cock pressing against them, and tried to go to sleep, thinking about what had just happened.

The following morning we arose bright and early, showered, dressed and got ready to fly off to the island of Mykonos. After having breakfast in the hotel dining room, Dimitri arrived to take us to the airport. He greeted us enthusiastically but I noticed that he never mentioned anything about the previous night. It was almost as if nothing had happened.

We loaded our luggage into the car and Brad said, sarcastically, "I think you ought to sit in the front, Joe."

I felt a little embarrassed, but climbed into the front seat next to Dimitri, who turned and smiled at me, and off we went to the airport. When we had arrived at the airport and unloaded the luggage, Dimitri shook our hands to say goodbye and then turned to me and said, "If you need anything, here is my telephone number – just phone me."

I shook his hand and felt his firm clasp around my hand. We thanked him for his kindness in showing us around Athens and told him we would probably see him on our return in about two weeks' time. We then bade him farewell and made our way through the airport to the plane to take us on the relatively short flight to Mykonos.

CHAPTER 2

MYKONOS

The flight to the island of Mykonos didn't take long. Although we were crammed into a relatively small plane, the flight itself was comfortable and as there were no hunky flight stewards to ogle at, so much of our time was spent looking out of the windows of the plane at the turquoise sea below. There was very little conversation except if we noticed a small island below us then we would inform the others. However, there was a sense of excitement as we neared the island of Mykonos. We flew over the barren island, surrounded by the bluest of seas, and landed at the small airport. Once we had disembarked, we caught a rickety bus from the airport which took us to Mykonos Town, and as we exited from the bus terminus, we were greeted by a number of locals selling accommodation to those who had not booked any in advance, which we had not done. Each of these people carried a photo album depicting their particular accommodation, making the selection of accommodation quite an experience. It became quite a battle as each tried to outdo the other. The chatter from the locals sounded like a flock of birds fighting over a piece of food. Clint didn't want anything to do with this, so he left the decisions to Brad and me. Naturally, the two of us spent most of this time admiring the handsome young men gathered around, rather than looking at the photos they had on offer. We did, however, realize that with all the other passengers from the flight also possibly searching for accommodation, we would have to make a decision quickly or we would have nowhere to stay.

A young, olive-skinned boy who looked about eighteen years old with straight, black hair thrust his photo album in front of us. We both looked up to see who had thrust this book under our noses. His face was bronzed and smiling and his body looked lithe and fit. On seeing the young boy, we looked at each other, and I think we knew what the other was thinking.

"We need accommodation for three," said Brad, taking the initiative.

"Is it for you three?" he asked pointing at us, smiling broadly.

"Yes," replied Brad, "but we don't have to have separate rooms, we can share the same room."

"I think I can offer you something," said the youth, now beaming broadly at us.

He told us where the accommodation was in relation to the layout of the main town, Chora or Mykonos Town, and gave us the price per night. Brad and I went into a little huddle to discuss the offer and more importantly, the potential of the young man, and then we turned to him and said, "We like what we see so we'll take it."

He seemed delighted and led the way to a rather old, rickety vehicle that looked more like a motorized tricycle. He took our luggage, threw it into the small cart at the back and said, "Come, we go."

"Hang on!" shouted Clint. "What do you mean we go? There isn't room for all of us to fit into this thing."

"That's right," replied the youth, grinning, "that is why I take the luggage and you walk."

This came as a shock to us. Clint turned in anguish to Brad and said, "What if he steals our luggage?"

"Don't worry," said Brad, "I'll travel with him on the motorcycle part and you two can walk to his place. I'll see that he doesn't go too fast so that you can keep up with us."

Clint and I just stood there dumbfounded while Brad gleefully leapt onto the only available seat and held onto the young man for dear life. The motorcycle roared into life and off they went, Brad waving to us as Clint and I ran as fast as we could, trying to keep up with the vehicle so that we didn't lose sight of them.

Although the streets, if you can call them that, in Mykonos Town, are extremely narrow, we didn't have to run too far before we reached a quaint whitewashed building with a ginger cat lying outside in the shade. By the time we arrived there, Brad and the youth had off-loaded the luggage and were waiting for us. Clint and I came panting along the street, glaring at Brad, who had traveled in relative luxury.

To me, all the buildings on Mykonos seemed to look the same, so until I went into the building outside which they stood, I wasn't sure whether this was the same building that we had seen in the photo album.

"Thanks, Vasilis," I heard Brad say.

So that's what the youth's name was. Then I thought to myself, Brad certainly didn't waste any time getting to know the youth. We took our luggage into the building and were pleasantly surprised to see how clean and comfortable the front room looked and how pleasantly cool it was once inside of the building.

Vasilis called in Greek for someone, and a middle-aged woman, whom I presumed to be his mother, came into the room. They spoke to each other, and then she nodded and smiled at us and then reverted back to speaking Greek with Vasilis. As we didn't speak Greek, we had no idea as to what was being discussed. Eventually, she gave us another smile and disappeared into what we presumed must be the kitchen. Vasilis picked up one of the bags and motioned for us to follow him. We went through a doorway, down a short corridor and come into a room with a double bed against one of the walls. The only other features in the room were a wash-hand basin and a cupboard in which to put our clothes. In one of the other walls was a door.

"Is that the bathroom through there?" I asked.

"No," replied Vasilis, "that's my room. The bathroom is outside in the back. In the front room, where you came in, is where we eat. You will get breakfast, but that is all."

For the price that we were paying, none of us was going to complain. It was cheap but clean, and we had decided, that is, Brad and me, without any discussion between us, that the owner's son was very good looking and that in itself would make up for anything that was lacking in this home.

We unpacked our bags, hung our clothes in the cupboard and set off to discover this exciting town.

The narrow streets are protected from both the wind and sun, and are paved with flagstones, which are whitened, making the streets feel cool. At the intersections of the streets, small irregular squares are formed, also serving as forecourts to some of the many churches that one finds on Mykonos. We wandered around, occasionally getting lost until we eventually found ourselves in the harbor area. There were quaint crowded open-air tavernas along the waterfront and little fishing boats bobbing in the harbor. The whole picture was one of enjoyment and tranquility; precisely like we had seen in the travel brochures. That evening we were to see how this tranquility would change.

As is the case with so many European countries, after a leisurely lunch at one of the tavernas, we found our way back to our new home and the three of us climbed onto our double bed to have an afternoon sleep.

"Now this is what I call civilization," quipped Brad.

"Meaning?" asked Clint.

"Well after you've had a good meal, the last thing you feel like doing is work; so it makes sense that they all have a sleep in the afternoon."

"Shut up you two, I want to sleep," I chirped, closing my eyes and drifting into the quiet slumbers of sleep.

In the early evening, I awoke and went into the front room of our "home" to see if Vasilis was there as I wanted to find out where the "in" places were on Mykonos. I found him sitting shirtless in a pair of shorts reading a magazine. I stared at his young, yet muscular, body, admiringly, and smiled at what I saw.

"Vasilis, I'm sorry to worry you, but where do people on the island go in the evening?"

He put down his magazine, looked up at me and flashed a smile, which revealed a beautiful set of white teeth which contrasted beautifully against his tanned skin.

"That depends on what you want," he replied, with a twinkle in his eyes. "On Mykonos, anything goes and we cater for everyone."

I wasn't quite sure how to take that statement. "Well, we'd like to go and have a nice dinner and then maybe go to a club or bar."

"There are a few clubs but many more bars near the waterfront," he said. "If you would like, I can take the three of you and show you, tonight."

"If you're not doing anything tonight, we'd be very grateful. What time shall we meet you?"

"It's no good going for dinner before ten o'clock, because it is still too light, and nothing much happens before midnight."

"Don't you people ever sleep, except during the day?" I joked.

He laughed. "Only sometimes," he retorted.

I liked him because not only was he good-looking, but at least he had a sense of humor. I then went back to the room to find that the other two were now awake.

"Where have you been?" asked Clint.

"Chatting up Vasilis!" I replied with a twinkle in my eyes.

I noticed how Brad stared at me. "You're not serious are you?"

From that look, I wondered if he was jealous.

"I'm only joking. I've been asking him where one goes here at night?"

Brad looked a little relieved and I thought that there might be something between him and Vasilis.

"So where are we going?" he asked.

"Vasilis said he would take us around the town and show us the sights," I told them.

Not knowing what our new, young friend was planning for us, we showered and readied ourselves for the evening. There was a knock on the inter-leading door to Vasilis's room and he entered. He was dressed all in white. He had on a white vest that hugged his naturally defined torso and a pair of tightly fitting white jeans. The whiteness seemed all the brighter because of his tanned, olive-colored skin. All three of us stood in awe and stared at this vision.

"You look terrific," said Brad, spontaneously. I don't really think he knew what to say, but felt he had to say something.

"Thank you," replied Vasilis, showing those pearly-white teeth again. "You are ready?" he questioned.

"Yes, we're ready," Clint replied, and the four of us left for a night out on the town.

If you have never visited Mykonos, I can tell you that it has vibes! There are beautiful people everywhere, and each new person you see, seems more beautiful than the last. They are all well-tanned from the summer sun and wear the skimpiest of clothing to show off their developed and defined bodies.

We wandered the busy streets filled with people and then found a taverna on the waterfront where we had the most delicious dinner of lamb, Greek salad and Retsina wine. The lamb and the salad were easy to digest, but the Retsina took some getting used to with its biting, acidic flavor. However, after a while, we had consumed so much of the rather sharp tasting wine that the taste didn't bother us. From there we set off for one of the clubs that Vasilis was going to take us to.

When we got to the club, there were people milling around in the streets and the music was thumping inside. We paid and went in. The place was dark, but with the lighting that was being used, you could see that the dance floor was packed with bodies, some dressed and some half undressed, obviously because of the heat. We managed to find a table to sit at and Vasilis went off to order drinks for us. Brad immediately followed – to give him a hand to carry the drinks, he had said. When they returned, we sat drinking and trying to talk over the noise of the music. People danced with whoever was available. There were men with men, women with women and men dancing with women. Nobody seemed to mind or take any notice.

Brad plucked up the courage and shouted over the noise of the music, "Do you want to dance, Vasilis?"

"Sure!" came the gleeful answer, and off they went to the dance floor.

We watched Brad and Vasilis enjoying themselves and then I looked at Clint and said, "Come on, let's dance," and so off we went.

We all took turns in dancing with each other and generally had a wonderful evening together. It must have been about three in the morning when Clint and I said that we were tired and were going home, but Brad still had plenty of energy to carry on with Vasilis.

We walked through the cool streets of Mykonos to the house. When we got home, I stripped off my clothes and fell onto the bed, exhausted. I lay there with my eyes closed listening to Clint take his clothes off and get ready for bed. I felt him get onto the double bed, but it felt as if he wasn't lying on the bed. I lay there for a while, when suddenly I felt a warm breath over my stomach. I didn't move, but then I felt Clint's tongue lick the top of my cock. It felt so good and warm. He then wrapped his mouth around my cock and slowly worked his way down my shaft, getting me harder all the time. He kept this up for quite a while until I was fully hard and then I decided to reciprocate. I crawled under him so that my mouth could reach his huge cock, and I started working on him.

Clint had a reputation for being large in every aspect, and taking him in any position needed total relaxation. I relaxed my throat and slurped his dick into my throat until I could feel my nose hitting his balls. We were both enjoying this when the bedroom door leading to the corridor opened. We froze. I opened my eyes and in the light from the corridor, I could see it was Brad and Vasilis. Obviously, the light from the corridor also lit us up so that they could see what we were doing. Clint just carried on sucking me as though nothing had happened once he knew who it was. Vasilis and Brad came into the room and closed the door behind them. I heard them getting undressed, or undressing each other and then I felt the bed move as they both got onto the bed together. In the meantime, Clint and I had carried on enjoying what each of us had to offer the other.

I felt Clint lean off the bed and then move his position. I heard foil tearing and knew that someone was getting a condom – I assumed it was Clint. He continued working on my cock then I felt him between my legs. His tongue was moving everywhere, creating excitement through my body. I heard another foil being torn and assumed that Brad or Vasilis was preparing to put on a condom. I put out my hand to feel who was next to me. From the feel of the chest and body, I was sure it was Vasilis. My hand wandered lower until it touched his erect cock. I knew Brad's cock well, and this didn't feel like his, so it must be Vasilis lying next to me.

I heard Vasilis gasp as Brad entered him, and I squeezed his cock as if to let him know it would all be fine. Just then I felt the hardness of Clint's barge-pole about to enter me. I relaxed because I knew what to expect. He was very gentle because he was aware of his size, and allowed me to slide onto him, rather than push into me. Both Vasilis' and my legs were in the air while Brad was sliding in and out of Vasilis, and Clint was doing likewise to me.

From the movement on the bed, you could tell that all four of us were working as a team. Brad and Clint seemed to be in unison sliding in and out of us, while we lay there groaning and moaning in ecstasy. Eventually, Clint's rhythm increased and I knew that he was close to coming. Brad felt the change in movement on the bed and he increased his pace – they obviously wanted to come together. Clint gave a deep growl, which I knew to be the sign, and he began shooting his load into me. As he did so, I let fly with my load and gripped Vasilis' cock, working it faster and faster. He gave a little cry and I felt the wetness shoot over my hand as he unloaded his supply. In doing so, his asshole muscles clamped tightly around Brad's cock and Brad fired his load into Vasilis. When it was all over and our breathing had returned to normality, Brad collapsed on top of Vasilis, while Clint did likewise with me and that is how we found ourselves when we awoke hours later.

CHAPTER 3

THE SHEPHERD BOY

Today, we decided to take ourselves to the beach to have a taste of nudity that Brad had told us about. A sense of excitement built up within us as we headed towards the bus station; after all, it wasn't every day that we had the opportunity to parade naked in public.

We caught the old, rickety bus fairly early from Mykonos Town to the beach of Platys Yalos from where we would catch a boat to Super Paradise beach. This was going to be Brad's day of naked men and decadence, if what the guide book had said was true. The bus trip was in itself an education because we were required to give the driver the exact cost of the journey as he told everyone he had no change, so if you offered him more than the price of the journey, then it was his lucky day. The other interesting fact was that the bus never left until the driver thought he had enough passengers, so any thought of a timetable went out of the window, so to speak. The bus, packed with seated and standing passengers, bumped its way along the gravel road, throwing up large clouds of dust behind it. Once we reached Platys Yalos, we all boarded our small boat and chugged across the azure sea stopping at a few small beaches on our way, to offload those tourists who wished to stay at that particular beach. When we arrived at Super Paradise, there were quite a few people there already. We jumped from the boat and found ourselves a section of space on the beach, and put down our towels and peeled off our clothes – after all, this was a nudist beach. We oiled our bodies with suntan lotion and lay down on the soft sand to absorb the sun's rays. The sun beat down upon us with intense heat and after about fifteen minutes in the sun, we had to dive into the crystal clear sea to cool down. The sea was a savior to us because it refreshed our hot bodies as the only other type of cooling was a bit of shade which came in the form of some slatted bamboo shelter from the taverna situated on the beach. The three of us frolicked in the tranquil, clear waters enjoying its refreshing coolness and each other's company. It was so relaxing to bob up and down in the gentle swells in the sea as we floated around in between our frolicking.

After having spent some time in the sun as well as in the sea, I ventured to go exploring over the barren countryside, to see what other life there might be at the top of the cliffs. Brad said that he wanted to go for a walk as well, so the two of us set off leaving Clint to look after our towels and clothes. We climbed the rugged rock-face, which had led down to the beach, passing lizards that sunned themselves on rocks and then scuttled off when we approached, possibly because of our nakedness. The only things that Brad and I had on were sandals to keep the heat from our feet; other than that, we were naked, slowly being burnt by the sun. Eventually we reached the top of the cliff that overlooked the beach. The view from there was superb. The sea was a clear azure and there was only a gentle lapping on the seashore. We looked down onto the beach and saw all the naked bodies lying there. Up at the top of the cliff, there was silence – no chatter reached our ears from those on the beach and as there were no waves crashing, the sea sounded silent as well. As we stood at the top of the cliff, Brad saw a stone building approximately a kilometer from where we were.

"I think I'm going to take a walk over there and see what it is," he said.

"OK," I replied, "I'm going to walk along the edge of the cliff and if it gets too hot, I'll come over to the stone building to get some shade."

I set off along the cliff edge and watched Brad head towards the stone building. As I walked along, I could see beautiful, secluded coves that could only be reached by boat. I found one spot that I couldn't resist. I stopped walking and sat down and looked down at the most tranquil beach I had ever seen. It was completely sheltered from the other beaches with snow-white sand and placid water – in fact the water was so still, it resembled a swimming pool, and not a soul inhabited the beach. It was a pity that I couldn't get down to that beach from the top of the cliff.

I must have sat there for some time because I could feel the sun beginning to burn me, so I decided that it was time for me to get into some shade before I suffered from sunstroke. I turned and headed towards the stone building that Brad had gone to. As I neared it, I could see that it must be some sort of shepherd's shelter. It had a doorway, without a door, and an opening, which represented a window. As I neared the window I could see that it was fairly dark inside so I knew that it had a roof on it to offer some shade. I got to just outside of the window when I heard heavy breathing coming from the inside of the building. I crept up to the window opening and gingerly peered through. The first things that I saw as I looked through were some clothes lying on the floor, I knew that Brad had no clothes on, so it had to be someone else in there. As I peered further in through the opening of a window, I saw the back view of Brad, crouching over somebody with that person's cock in his mouth. I could also see that the other person had Brad's cock in his mouth and that they were sucking each other off. There was much muffled moaning and grunting as they attacked each other as though this was the last meal they were ever to have. I stayed glued at the window opening, watching the two with fascination. I looked at the clothes again and decided they looked of the quality that a shepherd boy might wear – a little worse for wear.

The two of them seemed lost in their own world, until the shepherd boy came close to releasing his load. He let go of Brad's cock for a moment, said something in Greek, went back to Brad's cock to work on it with haste, and then proceeded to shoot his young cum down Brad's throat. Brad never let go, nor did the shepherd boy, when Brad let out a grunt and shot one load after another down this young throat. Both of them continued to milk each other dry just as they might have been doing to the goats that the shepherd boy should probably have been looking after. After Brad had come, he rolled from the young boy and lay on the cool earth next to him, both panting from exhaustion. I remained outside the window, without them seeing or hearing me. I heard the young boy saying something in Greek and begin to get dressed, and then I heard his footsteps as he left the building. Silently, I made my way round to the doorway and stood there smiling at Brad who was still lying in the shade.

"You been here long?" he said, leaning on his elbows.

"Oh, just long enough to get a hard-on watching you two at it," I said. "Where did you find him?"

"When I came into the building, he was in the corner, playing with himself."

"So you decided not to let him play alone!"

"Oh shut up, Joe. He was obviously very frustrated because he didn't stop when I came in, nor did he seem embarrassed to be doing it in front of me."

I walked over to Brad and offered him a hand to pull him up off the floor, "It's just that he couldn't resist a good thing when he saw it," I joked.

I pulled him up and he playfully punched me on the arm. "I'll get you back," he said putting his arm around my shoulder. "Come on, we'd better get back before Clint thinks something has happened to us."

"I think you'd better wait until that huge cock of yours has subsided a bit or people might think you and I have been at it," I replied, also wanting to get rid of my hard-on.

We waited just long enough for Brad and me to lose our erections and then we headed back to the beach. We wound our way back to our towels and didn't see Clint, and then we found him sitting at the taverna in the shade.

"I suppose you guys have been busy again," he said, sarcastically, with a glint in his eyes.

"No," I replied, "only this guy," I said, pointing to Brad.

"And who was it this time?" enquired Clint, not allowing himself to be discouraged.

"A shepherd boy," I laughed.

"As long as it wasn't the sheep," replied Clint light-heartedly.

I could see that at last, Clint was beginning to relax a little, but we needed to get him to 'let his hair down'.

We had a very pleasant lunch at the taverna where we laughed and chattered away, filling Clint in on what had happened up on the top of the cliff, until we decided we had enjoyed enough sunshine for one day so we took the first boat back to Platys Yalos and then continued on to Mykonos Town, once more, by rickety bus.

We eventually arrived back at our residence, looking tanned but exhausted and spent the rest of the afternoon sleeping. We woke up to knocking on the inter-leading door to Vasilis' room.

"Come in," I shouted and Vasilis came in.

"I can see that you've had a good day at the beach," he said, "but you must be careful of the sun."

We were very grateful for this information, but it was a little late as we had already experienced the viciousness of the sun.

"You must rub some cream on your sunburn," suggested Vasilis.

As we never had any, we didn't comment on his suggestion.

"Do you not have any?" enquired Vasilis, "because I can get you some."

"Would you mind?" I asked, thinking that he might have to go and buy some from one of the stores.

"Of course. We always have in case of tourists like you," he laughed.

"What do you mean, 'tourists like us'?" responded Brad.

"Well, you always go in the sun too long and then you burn and suffer. You must tan gradually, then you too will have the color skin like I have," said Vasilis, lifting his shirt to show us his tan, and obviously his trim, tight stomach muscles.

Vasilis hastened off to get some cream and soon returned with a small jar of cool, refreshing cream, which we rubbed onto ourselves.

"We thought we might go out to a bar or club tonight," said Brad, "and we wondered if you'd like to come with us."

"Of course; I will show you around. Do you want to go drinking or would you like to go and watch a movie?"

I laughed.

"You have movies here on Mykonos?" I asked, not really believing that they did.

"You seem surprised that I say we have films here. We have an open-air theatre where we see the films."

"Open-air!" Exclaimed Clint, "But the sun never seems to set so what time do they have movies here?"

"You're right about the sun, but if we're lucky, it might start around 11:00pm."

"So late?" asked a stunned Brad.

"Well you must understand that it is too light if it is open-air," replied Vasilis, good-humidly.

"Hey, guys, why don't we try it? At least when we go back home we can brag about watching open-air movies at midnight because the sun hadn't set yet," I joked.

And so it was agreed that we would go for drinks and then dinner followed later by movies.

We later showered and pulled on some casual clothes and, together with Vasilis, we set off into the heart of Mykonos.

The drinks were pleasant as we sat near the water's edge at the harbor and dinner was equally pleasurable with a delicious lamb dish and Greek salad, followed by more drinks, including a bottle of rather stringent Retsina wine.

"Yuk!" was Brad's reaction to the Retsina, which brought tears of laughter from Vasilis.

"It is an acquired taste," said our young host.

"It's like drinking paint thinners," commented Clint.

"Have some more," said Vasilis encouragingly, "The more you drink the easier it becomes to enjoy."

"Never!" replied Brad. "The more I drink, the more my throat feels like someone's grated it and dried it out."

We never got to finish the bottle of wine because the taste was too astringent, but the company made up for the wine.

After dinner, we wandered the narrow streets of Mykonos town, looking at the shops which were still doing a roaring trade, and watching the people. That's a favorite pastime at many of the Greek islands: people watching.

As the sun set and the glow over the horizon began to fade, we set off to where Vasilis had said the cinema was. By this time it was well past 10:00 in the evening, but the streets were thronging with locals and tourists alike.

We bought our tickets to the movie and went in. I say went in, not to a building but rather a four-walled shell. It resembled what might have been a very large building that had the roof removed and all interior walls demolished. What stood there were the four exterior walls and what the locals had done was placed rows and rows of benches on the floor all facing the wall opposite the entrance or front door. The sky became the roof and that was why we had to wait for darkness before they could start the film.

There was a sense of excitement. Young children ran hither and thither, playing games, while the adults indulged in their favorite drink in plastic mugs, chatting to one another. As for the four of us, well we also joined in the excitement and novelty of the occasion by getting ourselves something to drink, found a bench and waited with anticipation for the movie to start.

There was no build up to the main movie, like shorts or forthcoming attractions; we went straight into the film which was in English but with Greek sub-titles. The drinks flowed throughout the movie and by the time it ended, which was around 12:30 the following morning, we and all the other members of the audience were very merry and ready to party the night away.

CHAPTER 4

A RELAXING DAY

After our interesting night out at the movies and getting back to Vasilis's home at around 3:00 in the morning, we spent most of the rest of the morning sleeping. At around 11:30a.m I awoke to hear the shower running. Clint was up but Brad was still sprawled out next to me in the bed. I watched as his chest rose and fell gently as he breathed and I admired his physicality. I couldn't resist touching his chest as he breathed and so I laid my hand on it and watched my hand rise and fall on his chest. As I did this, I became aware of how aroused I'd made myself and wondered if I should go a little further and slide my hand down his firm stomach. I didn't need much thought, because temptation got the better of me and my hand began a slow journey over his abs and tight stomach to his pelvis and then I felt it: his cock was erect and hard. Gently I ran my fingertips along the shaft until I reached his balls which I gently cupped in my hand and gave a gentle squeeze.

"Hey! What are you after?" came a grunt and groan from Brad, and he turned to face me, smiling.

"Are you horny?" I asked quietly.

"Am I ever horny?" was the reply.

"Always! It's just that I was wondering…"

"Wondering whether you could slip in or not, I suppose?"

I giggled and Brad started tickling me until we were like two school girls rolling around on the bed 'fighting'.

"What the hell are you two up to?" asked Clint emerging from his shower, drying himself.

"Joe was trying to get my ass and I was putting a stop to it," answered Brad.

"Crap," came the resolute reply. "You never stop anyone from getting your ass," continued Clint, like a reprimanding father-figure. "Now tell me, you two horny men, what we're doing today."

We stopped our fun on the bed and lay there panting from exhaustion.

"I don't know," I said, thinking for a while. "Maybe go to the beach."

"And you Brad?" asked Clint.

"Maybe the same."

And so by a democratic decision of two votes, we decided to head to the beach.

We caught our regular rickety bus to Platys Yalos and then the boat to Super Paradise beach where we disembarked. The beach was pretty full and people were already enjoying lunch in the small taverna, so finding a spot of vacant beach was somewhat tricky, but we managed to get a piece of beach down near the water's edge. It was handy being there because it meant when we got excessively hot, we could virtually roll into the water and cool off, but if we wanted to venture up the rock face and walk along the cliff edge, or even head to Brad's shepherd hut, we'd have to make our way through the crowds taking up space on the sandy beach. Not that this was a problem as it allowed us to survey all the naked bodies on display.

We placed our towels on the sand, stripped off and helped each other put on suntan lotion until our naked bodies glistened in the sun. There were naked bodies scattered all around and some, who were taking strain in the sun, were frolicking in the cool, crystal waters of the Aegean Sea.

The beach itself was not large and therefore it made it necessary for there to be close proximity with other people who were tanning. This meant that one could hold a quiet conversation with another tourist who might be six or seven inches away from you. It was just this situation that got Clint chatting to a guy who said he was from Germany and was lying next to Clint.

I could see how friendly they had become and that whenever Clint went for a swim to cool off, the German, whose name we established was Heinz, also went. Both Brad and I nudged each other the first time Clint and his new friend went for a swim.

"Do you think there's something brewing there?" asked Brad as he watched the two dive into the cool sea.

"Who knows? Maybe something might come of it, but it might only be a beach chat, if you know what I mean."

"Wait and see if they go up the cliff and then disappear."

"Maybe we should tell Clint where the shepherd's hut is," I suggested to Brad.

"At least their asses and cocks won't get burned in the blazing sun," replied Brad.

I laughed out loud.

"Trust you to think of something like that."

When the two came back from their swim and Clint dropped back onto his towel, dripping water on us, Brad suggested that if he intended to 'go for a walk', to look for the shepherd's hut.

"What do you mean 'go for a walk" asked Clint?

Obviously, we couldn't say too much with Heinz lying so close to us.

"You know…," I hinted, looking in the direction of the top of the cliff.

Clint looked in the direction in which my eyes went then returned to look at me, but with a bewildered expression. Brad giggled when he saw Clint's expression.

"You know, Clint, sometimes you can be so slow. Joe was suggesting that if you and you know who decided to go for a walk to do you know what, then there is a small shepherd's hut where you can go and there's shade."

Clint gave us both an indignant look which brought forth more giggles from us.

After at least another half an hour of enduring the blazing sun, Clint slipped on his shoes and said he was going for a walk. He stood up, his long cock swinging freely in the sun and headed up the cliff. It wasn't two minutes later and Heinz had also risen and was heading off in the same direction as Clint. Brad and I grinned a knowing grin to each other and continued to enjoy the warmth of the sun.

During Clint's absence, Brad and I went in for a swim a number of times, in an effort to cool down. Eventually both Clint and Heinz returned, together. Both were chatting quite comfortably with each other and they seemed to have an air of contentment about them. They both lay down on their respective towels and smiled to each other, but neither Brad nor I said anything.

It wasn't until we were on the boat heading back to Platys Yalos to catch the bus back to Mykonos Town, that we broached the topic of Clint's walk.

"So, tell us all," said Brad with a smirk across his face.

"About what?" replied a somewhat contrite Clint?

"You and Heinz," I added. "Do you like him?"

"Yeah, he seems quite a decent sort of guy," answered Clint, without making any effort to elaborate.

"And...!" resumed Brad, hoping to get every drop of juicy scandal from Clint.

"We made out, up on the cliff," replied Clint curtly.

Brad beamed when he heard this.

"So what's he like?" continued Brad.

This was like drawing blood from a stone, except the stone had dried up. When we arrived at Platys Yalos and had disembarked, Clint sat almost ignoring us and staring out of the bus window as we headed back home.

"Are you meeting him tonight?" resumed Brad, after there had been a long period of silence.

"Yes," replied Clint. "And I'm having dinner with him as well."

This came as a bit of a shock to us as although we had never agreed to always have dinner together, it was an unwritten idea that we would, and now Clint was not going to be with us. It didn't really worry me, but it did worry Brad. Brad's face was a picture of shock and disbelief. I could see that he didn't know what to say next, so I decided I'd speak up.

"That's great Clint. Are you guys planning anything after dinner? What I mean is do you want us out of the way for the two of you tonight?"

"I don't know. Heinz and I will play it by ear after dinner, but you guys go out and do whatever you're planning to do."

For the rest of the journey Brad remained silent; in fact I'd never known him to be speechless. Added to this, I had never really known Clint to be so private, although if I thought about it, he never bragged about his conquests in the manner that Brad did. When we returned to Vasilis's house, we all showered to get the sea salt off our bodies and then lay down to have a rest before we all ventured out in the evening.

I awoke from my afternoon rest at about 7:00p.m and both Cline and Brad were still asleep. The sun was still blazing down and I could still feel the intense heat when I strolled outside. Neither Vasilis nor his mother was about, so I sat in their lounge rather than stay out in the sunshine. I must have sat there for about an hour, when Clint then emerged and joined me. I wasn't sure whether I should broach the subject of his new friend, Heinz, so instead we made small talk and I left it to him if he wanted to say anything about Heinz. Nothing was said about Heinz. Soon Brad also joined us having just woken up.

"So what's happening tonight?" asked Brad, as though it was the first time that this topic was being discussed.

Both Clint and I looked at him bewilderedly.

"Brad, weren't you listening to Clint on the boat and the bus?" I asked, shaking my head in disbelief.

"I just thought he was having us on."

Clint then shook his head in disbelief.

"Okay, okay! I get it. So does that mean you and I are going out together, Joe?"

"Sure, if you want my company?"

"Of course I do, seeing my other friend doesn't."

I still sensed that Brad was a little upset, but I wasn't going to continue the topic of Clint's date for the evening.

We all went back to our room to get dressed for the evening and while we were getting ready, Vasilis came in.

"Where have you been?" I asked.

"Shopping with my mother. Are you guys going out?"

"Yeah. Do you want to join us," remarked Brad, "because Clint won't be with us; he's got a date."

"That's nice, Clint," said Vasilis. "Where you going?"

"Just out for dinner," answered Clint.

"Just dinner!" was the snide comment from Brad. "I think there might be more than dinner tonight, Vasilis."

"So what if there is. That is good for Clint. You must always try to have dessert after dinner, you know; it makes for a satisfying evening," said Vasilis with a glint in his eye.

Clint smiled broadly at Vasilis's comment, and I saw for the first time that day, Clint's pleasure.

"Well, listen. If we're all going in different directions tonight, and there might be a possibility that Clint won't be home tonight, what are we going to do tomorrow?" asked Brad.

There was silence at first and then Brad continued.

"I was thinking of going to Delos tomorrow," said Brad. "Do you think it's worthwhile visiting, Vasilis?"

Vasilis looked seriously at us and then said, "It depends what you are looking for?"

"I thought that historically it was worth a visit," I said.

"Oh yes, it is, but there's more there than just history," he answered. "That is the place of Apollo," he continued, almost whispering the last comment.

"Yes, I know," I replied. "Delos is reputed to be the birthplace of Apollo. According to Homer, in Greek mythology, Leto, exhausted with labor pains, looked for somewhere to give birth to the child she had begot with Zeus, and so Apollo was born on the island," I rattled on, sounding like a tour guide, thanks to what I could remember from my studies.

"You seem to know something of our culture," said Vasilis, "but that is mythology. What I'm talking about is real."

"Well, I don't know what either of you are talking about," said Brad in desperation. "Are we going tomorrow?" he asked turning to Clint and me.

"If you want to go, you do so; I'm not into historical stuff," said Clint. "I feel like having a relaxing day doing a bit of shopping in the town or going to the beach again. I'll also see what Heinz feels like doing."

"And you, Joe?" asked Brad.

"I know I like historical things, but I also thought I'd like to go to the beach as well, but not necessarily with Heinz," I joked.

"If that's the way you feel, I'll go on my own," said Brad, reluctantly.

"If you do, please be careful," said Vasilis. "There are many old ruins there and it can be dangerous if you go off the beaten track."

"It looks pretty harmless to me, from what I've read in the books," retorted Brad, not about to be put off.

With that, it was the end of discussion on what was happening the following day. We all readied ourselves for a night out and set off in our various directions: Clint to meet Heinz and Brad, Vasilis and me to a bar, followed by dinner and clubbing.

When we arrived back from our evening out, Brad and I fell into bed and were soon fast asleep, oblivious of where Clint was and whether he was enjoying himself with Heinz.

The next morning when I got up, neither Brad nor Clint was in the bed, but Vasilis was. I rolled over in the bed and came face to face with a smiling Vasilis, who, when he saw me awake, scuttled to the base of the bed, burrowed his face in my crotch and began giving me an early morning blow-job. Trust me, there's nothing better than an early morning blow-job from a handsome young Greek boy who enjoys doing it as much as I enjoy receiving it.

"Where's everyone?" I asked when Vasilis's head finally popped up from between my legs and a satisfied smiled covered both our faces.

"I don't know. I haven't seen Brad or Clint; but I don't think Clint came home last night."

"Well, I'm not going to worry about them, I'm going to have breakfast and head off to the beach," I replied, hopping out of the bed and leaving Vasilis still lying there, smiling at my erection which bounced as I walked.

CHAPTER 5

AN EVENTFUL DAY IN PARADISE

I had eaten breakfast alone, packed a backpack with some water and some fruit to eat should I get hungry at the beach, caught the bus to Platys Yalos and then the boat and had arrived at Super Paradise beach to find very few people there, as it was still early. I found a spot next to some rocks, which allowed for some early morning shade, but I knew by midday I'd be roasting there. I stripped off and laid out my towel. Before lying down, I surveyed the people already there and didn't see Brad so I wondered if he'd gone to Delos Island or whether he'd gone shopping; either way, I was going to make the most of the sun and sea.

————————

Meanwhile, back in Mykonos Town, Clint was stirring in a foreign bed. He opened his eyes and looked at the young, yet heavily built German man lying next to him in the bed. Heinz opened his sleepy eyes and the two men smiled, lovingly at each other.

"Mornin'," said Heinz, moving closer to Clint and kissing him.

"Hi sexy! Did you sleep well?"

"I never had much choice, you were up all night and I don't mean awake and walking about."

Clint laughed as he knew that most of the night he'd certainly been erect and was pleasing both himself and Heinz.

"Do you never get enough?" queried Heinz.

"Not when I'm with a sexy man and especially one who encourages me for more."

"Well, do you want more?" asked Heinz, raising a quizzical eyebrow.

"That depends if you're able to take more," replied Clint, feeling his cock becoming aroused at the thought of fucking Heinz for the umpteenth time in one night.

Soon, both men were busy making love again as though this was their breakfast.

Back on the beach, I basked in the sun feeling it burning my body, until I felt the need to cool off in the sea. I rose from my towel and wandered to the water's edge, where a middle-aged man joined me.

"It's nice that there aren't so many people here yet," he said, dipping his feet into the water.

"Yes. At least you can find a spot to lie down in," I replied, wading into the sea until the water was up to my chest. "Come in, it's great."

The man followed me into the sea and soon he too was feeling the water's refreshing coolness. As we bobbed in the water, we started chatting and asking the usual touristy questions like; where are you from? How long are you staying here in Mykonos? Have you seen this and that? He said his name was Sven and he was from Sweden.

As we bobbed in the water, it was inevitable that occasionally our bodies touched and through the crystal clear water I could see that he had got himself an erection. Casually, I let my hand drift in the water until it brushed gently across his hard-on. Our eyes met and immediately, I got a hard-on. I felt his hand wrap around my shaft and he stroked it gently.

"That feels so good," he whispered, hoping no one would hear him.

I reciprocated by clamping my hand around his cock and he sighed as I did so.

"You do realize, Sven, that we can't get out of the sea now; not with us both aroused because everyone will see," I said, realizing the predicament we'd got ourselves into.

We both laughed and tried desperately to think of anything to deflate our cocks.

"Maybe we should take a walk, when we get out of the water," I suggested to Sven.

"You'll have to wait," he replied, "until I can get back to normal."

We were like two kids laughing and splashing because of our situation, but eventually, we were able to emerge from the sea with both cocks flaccid.

———————

Clint and Heinz had exhausted themselves once more and lay in each other's arms, panting gently as they returned to a state of relaxation.

"What are you planning on doing today?" asked Heinz.

"Whatever you feel like doing. I was going to go to the beach and maybe some shopping later this afternoon," replied Clint.

"That's OK by me," said Heinz rising from the bed and heading to the bathroom to shower. "Are you going to join me for a shower?" he shouted from the bathroom.

"Only if I can wash your back for you?" answered Clint.

"It's a deal," came the reply.

Soon the two men were under the cascading water, embracing each other. How much back washing was conducted leaves the mind boggling, but they were certainly exploring each other's body once again until they had both shot their load and had cleaned each other and finally come out of the shower and dried themselves.

Heinz packed a backpack for the beach and offered to lend Clint a towel as Clint had nothing for the beach with him. Together the two then set off for the beach. Although they traveled by bus to Platys Yalos like everyone else, they seemed to be floating with love, and when they eventually arrived at Super Paradise, they found themselves a spot and put down their towels, but in doing so, Clint had not seen me, as I was elsewhere.

I wandered up the rocks and paths from the beach, knowing that Sven was not far behind following the same route. My naked body, except for my sandals, was feeling the brunt of the blazing sun and I thought that maybe I should head for the shelter of the shepherd's hut and hope that Sven followed.

Once I reached the top of the cliff and turned around, I waited a little to allow Sven to see in which direction I was heading. He watched me and then followed, his long uncut cock swinging in the sunlight.

We walked until we reached the hut. I cautiously peered through the window opening and saw that the hut was empty so I went round to the doorway and went in. The pleasant coolness of the interior hit me and it was so welcoming to be in the shade. I moved to one of the corners and waited for Sven, who didn't take long to reach me.

"Thank goodness you have found shelter," he said as he made it into the coolness. "How did you know of this place?"

"I saw someone come here a few days ago when I was walking along the cliff," I replied, without elaborating on what I'd seen take place in the hut.

Sven walked up to me and put his arms around me and our lips met. I could feel my cock taking on a new life and becoming hard, but at the same time I felt Sven's cock jabbing my stomach. As our tongues explored each other's mouth, so our cocks rubbed up against each other and our passion increased. Soon we were down on the cool sand exploring each other's body. His mouth found my cock and began salivating along its length, and then I moved around so that I could take his long cock into my mouth. I watched as his foreskin slowly slid back to reveal his shiny cock head and then my tongue started lathering it.

"What do you like doing?" I asked Sven, when our mouths managed to let go of each other's cocks.

"I would very much like to fuck you, if you'll allow me," he politely asked.

It was so strange to hear someone ask politely when so often in the past guys merely said things like 'turn over I wanna fuck that ass of yours' or 'take my dick up your ass, fucker!'

I think it was just his manners and genteel politeness that made my mind up for me. I actually couldn't wait for Sven to sink his long cock into me, so I readied myself for his onslaught.

However before he slipped into my tight ass, I jokingly asked, "Are you going to rape and pillage me like a true Viking would?"

He roared with laughter at my suggestion and replied, "We have advanced, you know."

I felt the tip of his swollen cock press up against my asshole and then he slowly began to push forward. Gently and lovingly, he sank his shaft into my chute until his cock was buried to the hilt in me. A slow, rhythmic action started and soon we were both breathing rapidly as the passion increased.

Our positions changed all the time and throughout, our mouths searched for the others so that we could cement our passion. Although it was cool inside of the hut, the temperature was rising as we neared our climax and as if planned, we both shot our loads simultaneously, me covering Sven's stomach and chest with a fine layer of warm cum while he emptied his load into me, his cock throbbing with each discharge.

As we lay in each other's arms, allowing our bodies to cool down and to lose our erections, a feeling of contentment overcame both of us. There was no lasting love between us; it was sheer lustful passion that we had both desired and we'd achieved it. We eventually stood up and tried to clean Sven's chest and stomach before starting the journey down the cliff.

As we were half way down, Clint and Heinz were coming up the rocky path and we met mid-way.

"Hi there guys," I said jovially as we met.

Clint saw me with Sven and winked knowingly.

"Is Brad with you," asked Clint when we were alongside of each other.

"No. I don't know where he is. Maybe he's gone shopping or he might have gone to Delos."

"I'll see you back down there," replied Clint, continuing his journey up the cliff, no doubt to have fun with Heinz.

"Who was that?" enquired Sven.

"He's a friend that's traveling with me. We're staying at the same place."

"I thought it might be your boyfriend," continued Sven.

"Even if it was my boyfriend, he wouldn't have said anything because he was also with another guy."

When we reached the beach again, Sven thanked me and went his way to his towel and I to mine, as though we had never met. However, up on the top of the cliff, Heinz and Clint were exploring the barrenness of the countryside and each other.

Eventually the two exhausted young men returned and found me on the beach, where they joined me and we enjoyed the rest of the day swimming, tanning and exploring the upper reaches of the cliffs in search of pleasure.

CHAPTER 6

APOLLO

While Clint and I were having fun on Super Paradise beach, Brad had arrived at the little harbor on Delos, disembarked and wandered in an easterly direction towards the Agora of the Competaliastes. Inside the Agora, on his left, was the main road leading to the Sanctuary of Apollo. He headed along this road, together with a number of other tourists who had also caught the early morning boat. He continued to wander around the various ruins, seeing such beautiful mosaics as were found in the House of the Trident and the House of the Dolphins. The colors that have existed for centuries amazed him. To him it was incredible that these ruins and the artwork which existed within the ruins were still so beautiful. He wandered on, admiring what he saw.

He eventually found himself on his own, away from the other tourists and sat down on some stone ruins to take in what was around him. As he sat admiring the surrounding beauty, he heard tapping coming from behind an old wall. Out of curiosity, he rose and went to investigate. As he rounded the wall, he saw a man bent over some stone, tapping at it with a hammer. He had heard that there were archeologists on the island so he assumed this to be one of them.

He walked up to where the man was and greeted him, "Hi! I'm sorry to disturb you, but do you speak English?"

The man stopped what he was doing and looked up. He was probably about thirty years of age, well-tanned from being in the sun so much, and had well-developed arms, obviously from picking up heavy objects and from hammering. He was wearing a white vest and a pair of white shorts that revealed long, muscular legs.

"Yes, I do speak English. Although I am Greek, I studied archeology in England. Are you one of the day tourists?"

"Yes. I decided that I would like to come and see the ruins," Brad said.

The Greek was drawn to Brad almost immediately.

"There are many ruins here which are not open to the public, but I could show them to you, if you would like," replied the man, proudly.

"Thank you. Yes, I think I'd like that very much because I don't know my way around here, and it's not every day that you get to have your very own archeologist to guide you," Brad said smugly.

The man rose from where he had been crouching and hammering. As he did so, Brad could see that this young man had the body of a Greek God. It also seemed as though he had been poured into his shorts because it looked like there was no room for any of his muscles to fit into them. He had huge, rough hands from all the digging and hammering, but his face was unlined and handsome. He put down his hammer and proceeded to take Brad on a guided tour of the ruins.

They walked for many miles and saw many ruins and the man gave Brad detailed explanations on each of the ruins that they came across. Throughout this time, both Brad and the young Greek had passed admiring glances to each other.

They had wandered for some time when he asked Brad if he was thirsty. Naturally, Brad said that he was, as Delos is just like Mykonos, barren and extremely hot. They headed towards a remote building in the distance. There were no other buildings in the vicinity and Brad wondered whether this was also some ruin. As they neared it, Brad knew that it wasn't a ruin, but must be the archeologist's home while he worked on the island. It was a simple stone building, but it exuded charm among the barrenness of the island. They went into the coolness of the building where Brad's host offered him a glass of water. It amazed Brad how cool the interior was when compared to the intense heat outside.

"This is wonderfully cool in here," commented Brad.

"By the way, what is your name?" enquired the man.

"Brad and yours?"

"Apollo," he replied.

"That's a very appropriate name to have, especially as you are working on this island," replied Brad.

"I was given another Greek name, but I preferred to be called Apollo, so I chose to use that name instead."

"Well I think it's very appropriate, not only because of the link to the island, but I hope you don't mind me saying so, but I also think you look like a Greek God."

"Thank you for the flattery," he replied, smiling at Brad as he stood next to him. "It's very hot today, isn't it?" he said, taking off his vest to reveal a body that even Clint, who had done body-building, would have envied. Brad felt a stirring in his shorts as he stared at the muscular Apollo.

Apollo's body was chiseled, to say the least. His pecs were well-formed and rounded and his chest tapered down to a narrow waist and between the pecs and the waist was a set of rippling abdominal muscles; here was indeed a work of art.

"If you want to take off your top, you can do so," said Apollo.

Brad looked at Apollo's body and thought how small he must appear next to Apollo, and hesitated, but because it was so hot, he peeled off his T-shirt.

Apollo looked at him and put out a hand to touch Brad's chest. "I think you also have a very nice body. It's natural and well defined," he said, gently touching Brad's chest.

As Brad felt Apollo touch him, he also felt his cock getting extremely hard. He had never experienced anything like this before, a beautiful, muscular Greek man making a pass at him. He knew Clint was big, but this guy looked like a giant. Apollo's hand brushed across Brad's nipples and Brad let out a sigh. Brad also realized what I had said earlier before leaving home that Greek men were good looking.

"Do you like that?" asked Apollo.

"Yes," said Brad softly.

"Put your hands on my nipples and squeeze them gently," insisted Apollo.

Brad couldn't resist an invitation like that. He put his hands out in front of him and felt two firm pectoral muscles that had two hard nipples protruding from them. Through one of the nipples was a metal ring. He pinched them gently as he had been told to do and watched Apollo's reaction.

"That feels good," said Apollo, "but now you can squeeze them harder."

Brad squeezed a little harder but didn't want to hurt Apollo in case he became angry. Apollo still smiled.

"Harder," said Apollo. "Make me feel it. Pull on the ring."

Brad did as he was told.

"Put one of my nipples in your mouth and chew on it," instructed Apollo.

Brad was only too pleased to oblige. Brad leaned forward and took Apollo's left nipple into his mouth, sucked on it for a while and then placed it between his teeth and began to chew and grind on it, while at the same time, he pulled on the ring in Apollo's right nipple.

"Yes, that's more like it," growled Apollo, grinning wickedly with delight.

Brad could feel Apollo's warm breath against the back of his neck. Just then Apollo's right hand went to Brad's crotch and grabbed him between the legs and squeezed. Brad immediately let out a yell and let go of Apollo's nipple. He grimaced in pain as Apollo squeezed his balls and cock in his large hand. Apollo smiled as he saw Brad grimace.

"You feel hard," said Apollo, "you obviously like this."

Although Brad was in pain, he was amazed to realize that he was actually getting used to the pain. The grimace on his face began to disappear and he thought to himself that if Apollo could do that to him, he could do it back to Apollo. Brad's right hand went down to Apollo's crotch and he gripped Apollo's balls in his hand. Apollo stared at him almost in disbelief and said, "Did I say you could do that?"

Brad never expected him to say something like that and immediately let go.

"I'm sorry," apologized Brad.

"Come with me," said Apollo, still holding on to Brads crotch.

Apollo walked through the doorway into another room, dragging Brad behind him by the balls. When they entered the room, Brad's eyes nearly popped out of his head. Apollo closed the door behind them and let go of Brad's crotch. Brad looked around him. Against one wall was a rack with hooks attached to it, while hanging just off the center of the room was a leather sling attached to the roof by chains. Also hanging from the roof in another part of the room were some straps and in one corner of the room was what looked like a wooden bed, except it had no mattress on it. Brad had never been into whips and chains and seeing all this frightened him a little.

"You stay here," said Apollo, "and make yourself comfortable."

He then went out of the room again, locking the door behind him.

There was a small window in the room and this provided the only light for Brad. He wandered around the room looking at all the equipment. He moved to the sling in the center of the room and sat on it, and then he crossed over to the wooden bed. After a short time, the door was unlocked and Apollo entered. Brad stared once more in disbelief. There stood Apollo dressed only in a metal studded jock-strap, a hood over his face with openings for his eyes, nose and mouth, leather harness across his back and chest which had a cock-ring attached to a strap from the chest strap, and leather boots. Apollo's cock and balls had been placed through the cock-ring and because of the strap, his balls and cock seemed to be pulled up away from between his legs. Also attached to his nipple ring was a chain which led to his left nipple, which had a nipple-clamp, fastened to it. Apollo looked awesome. Brad's mind raced as he began to wonder what was in store.

"Slave!" commanded Apollo in a loud, deep voice, "get rid of your shorts."

Brad hesitated for a moment until he was shouted at once more by Apollo.

"Sure," said Brad, beginning to pull off his shorts.

"Yes, master!" commanded Apollo again.

Brad hesitated briefly, then quietly muttered, "Yes, master."

His shorts fell to the ground and for the first time, Apollo saw Brad in all his nakedness. He admired what he saw, but didn't show any emotions. Apollo crossed to where Brad stood and pushed him onto his knees so that Brad was at eye level to Apollo's crotch.

"Lick my boots," he ordered.

Brad felt the pressure being exerted on his head to bow lower, so he slowly lowered his head but wasn't sure whether he really wanted to do this. He hesitated, but Apollo forced his head further down.

Brad gently put his mouth to one of the boots, almost pretending to lick it.

"Lick it all the way up," shouted Apollo.

Brad put out his tongue and slowly began to work his way over the toecap and up the leg of the boot, which reached just below Apollo's knees. Apollo stood watching and Brad glanced up occasionally.

"Don't look at me," shouted Apollo.

Brad started tentatively licking Apollo's boots and once he'd become used to the texture of the leather and its taste, he continued licking his way up the boot until he reached the top of it. He wasn't sure what to do next, so he carried on up Apollo's leg. The taste of the boot contrasted with the taste of Apollo's sweaty flesh.

"I didn't say you could touch me," roared Apollo as he pushed Brad's head back down again. "I can see you need to be taught a lesson," he continued.

Apollo pulled Brad to his feet and marched him to the wall where the racks were situated. He attached Brad to the rack, making him face the wall and tying his hands to the top of the rack. He then spread Brad's legs and tied them to the lower part of the rack, and then he crossed to one of the other walls where some straps and whips were hanging. He selected a cat-o-nine-tails and moved back to Brad. Apollo stood a little way away from Brad and gently tickled Brad's back with the leather thongs of the cat-o-nine-tails. Brad held his breath as he felt the leather strips run across his skin. A strange erotic feeling ran through Brad's body. He could feel his cock throbbing and the gentle touch of the leather sent shivers of pleasure through him.

Apollo then started gently flicking them across Brad's back. Although it was not hurting Brad, every time they touched him, he flinched slightly. Slowly Apollo began to strike a little harder and this time, Brad began to emit sounds of pain whenever he was struck. The strange thing that Brad noticed was that, although he was enduring some pain, the more Apollo struck him, the more erect his cock became, and with every beating, his cock began to throb. Just as Brad was getting used to the whipping and the pleasure it was creating for him, so it stopped and he waited to see what was going to happen next.

He turned his head to see Apollo put down the cat-o-nine-tails and pick up a thick leather paddle. Brad's back had red marks across it, but the skin had not been broken. He then felt a whack from the paddle on his ass. It felt warm and reminded him of his school days when, on the odd occasion, he had received a hiding from the headmaster. The only difference was that when he was hit with the headmaster's cane, it had stung, but with the leather paddle, it seemed to give off a warm sensation. The strokes then became harder and Brad appealed to Apollo not to hit him so hard.

"I'll tell you when you may speak to me," said Apollo, continuing with the hiding.

Brad could feel tears beginning to well up in his eyes.

"Please," he sobbed, "no more, I'll do anything for you if you stop."

Although it was hurting, he was still feeling this warm feeling between his legs. He looked down at his cock and could see pre-cum beginning to ooze from the tip.

When Apollo felt that Brad had been disciplined enough, he stopped and untied him. When he turned Brad around to face him, he saw for the first time that Brad had been crying. He was the master, and therefore would not show any sympathy.

There was a bucket of water in one of the corners which Apollo picked up and splashed some of the water onto Brad's ass. Brad reacted to the coolness. Apollo took him by the arm and dragged him to the center of the room where the sling was situated. He positioned Brad in the sling, forcing his legs into the air and attaching them to the chains hanging from the roof. He then tied Brad's hands to the other chains so that Brad was now lying on his back in the sling with his arms and legs fastened in the air, but being able to move his head. Apollo walked over to the wall where the whips and other objects were, and picked up a long dildo that he smeared with some cream. He walked back to Brad and stood between Brad's legs, rubbing the end of the dildo against Brad's asshole. Brad tensed at first and waited for Apollo to make the entry, but it didn't happen. Instead, he felt the dildo being rubbed against his balls and then up and over his cock. Brad was beginning to enjoy this.

"Push it in," said Brad, who was enjoying the tantalizing touch of the dildo against him, but immediately Apollo removed the dildo from Brad's cock and balls.

"Don't tell me when to do things!" exploded Apollo.

"I'm sorry," whimpered Brad.

"I'm sorry, Master!" exclaimed Apollo loudly.

"I'm sorry, master," repeated Brad.

When Apollo felt he was ready, he positioned the head of the dildo against the entry to Brad's asshole and slowly pushed it in. Brad gave a deep sigh as it entered him. He tensed slightly, but as soon as he was used to it, he relaxed. Brad felt a glowing feeling run through his body as Apollo continued to push it further in and was amazed as to how far it had gone in before it wouldn't go any further. Seeing the dildo protruding from Brad had an influence on Apollo and his cock began to swell. He left the dildo sticking out of Brad and moved next to Brad's head. Brad opened his eyes and saw Apollo standing next to him. Apollo turned Brad's head sideways so that it was facing Apollo's crotch, which he moved closer to Brad's face.

"Eat it," he instructed, thrusting his crotch in Brad's face.

Brad could see the huge bulge in Apollo's leather jock-strap and opened his mouth. He wrapped his mouth around the studs on the jock-strap and the outline of Apollo's cock. He licked the leather and quite enjoyed the taste. He could feel how big Apollo's cock was from his running his mouth over the leather jock-strap He then became frantic trying to get Apollo's cock out of the leather pouch, and as he did so, Apollo started thrusting his pelvis towards Brad's face. Eventually from the movement, the tip of Apollo's cock appeared at the top of his jock-strap. Brad put out his tongue and started licking it.

"I didn't say lick it, I said eat it," shouted Apollo.

He suddenly unclipped the jock-strap, which fell to the floor and Brad was eye to eye with a large throbbing, cut cock. Apollo pushed his cock into Brad's mouth almost gagging him as he did so. Brad tried to pull his head away, but Apollo held him tightly so that he couldn't. Once Brad had got used to Apollo's cock going down his throat, he felt that he could handle the situation, after all, he realized that if he was to consider size, both his and Clint's cock were larger than Apollo's, but that was not to say that Apollo's was small, it was probably just fatter than his own. After some time of Apollo pounding into Brad's mouth, he pulled out and went back between Brad's legs. He first tried pushing the dildo further into Brad, and then started sliding it in and out of Brad's ass. With each push, Brad counter-pushed. Brad's cock was dribbling pre-cum down his cock stem and Apollo rubbed a finger in it and put it up to Brad's mouth.

"Suck it off," he said.

Brad wrapped his mouth around Apollo's finger and sucked. As he did so, Apollo started sliding his finger in and out of Brad's mouth. Both of them were now enjoying this.

Apollo suddenly pulled his finger from Brad's mouth and took hold of the dildo and slowly began to pull that out of Brad. As it exited, Brad gave a sigh and relaxed, but as he was doing so, he felt the top of Apollo's cock rub against his asshole. Apollo was not as gentle with his own cock as he was with the dildo, because he positioned it at Brad's asshole and just plunged straight in. Brad gasped. Apollo went all the way in and held it there.

Brad began to relax again, but before he was completely relaxed, Apollo was pounding into Brad's ass, pushing as far in as his cock could go and pulling out until the head nearly popped out, then pushing in again – this was hard fucking. Apollo held firmly onto Brad's legs causing the sling to swing to and fro. As a result of this swinging motion, he was able to pull Brad deeper onto his cock every time and so never lose his rhythm. This movement was getting Brad closer and closer to his climax until he could feel his balls moving up into his body, getting ready to explode. He lay there being pounded when suddenly he cried out, "Oh fuck, I'm going to come," and proceeded to shoot his hot, white cum all over his stomach. When Apollo saw this and felt Brad's ass muscles clamp around his own cock, his pounding became furious and fast. As he neared the moment that he was going to shoot his load, he pulled his cock out of Brad and shot over Brad's cock and stomach. He certainly carried a heavy load thought Brad, as he watched himself become covered in sticky cum.

When Apollo had finished shooting his load and his body had stopped jerking from the excitement, he rubbed his hand over their combined cum and then rubbed it over his own chest, coating his nipples in it. He then moved round to Brad's head, leant over him and said, "suck it off my nipples; we are now one."

Brad opened his mouth and ran his tongue over Apollo's nipples, taking in the salty flavors. When he had cleaned the cum from Apollo's nipples, Apollo undid the straps holding Brad's legs and arms and gently lifted him from the sling and carried him, like a baby, and placed him on the wooden bed, took off the hood covering his face, then he lay down next to him, put his arms around Brad and they both fell asleep.

CHAPTER 7

THE REVENGE

Once Clint and I returned to Vasilis's home, we showered and went shopping as we'd promised ourselves. That evening we had dinner together and went out for drinks as usual and then returned to our accommodation, without Heinz in tow and went to bed, exhausted from our tiring day.

"What are your feelings towards Heinz?" I asked as we lay side by side in the bed.

"I think he's a very nice guy," answered Clint, "but I was surprised how jealous Brad seemed that I was going out with Heinz."

I wasn't sure how to respond to that statement because I knew that Brad had some strong feelings for Clint, even though they weren't in a relationship.

"I think he just cares for you," I replied, "and doesn't want to see you hurt."

"No-one will hurt me," said Clint, confidently. "In any case, we said this was going to be a fun holiday, and I thought it was about time that I had some fun. Sure, Heinz was an amazing fuck and I could go to bed with him anytime, but I don't know that I would have a relationship with the guy."

"Why?"

"Joe, he's just a holiday fuck. For all I know he's probably got someone back in Germany waiting for him."

"Don't you think if he had someone, they would have come on holiday together?"

"Perhaps, but I just picked up a vibe that there might be someone in his life."

"Oh well, if anything is meant to happen between you guys, it will."

The following morning, I awoke early to yet another bright, sunny day. I got out of bed and saw that only Clint was in the bed with me. Perhaps Brad had returned late and spent the night with Vasilis in his room, or he had gone out while we were out and got lucky with someone else. I went through to the bathroom and when I returned to our room, I quietly opened the inter-leading door to Vasilis' room only to see him asleep alone in his bed. I went back to the bed and moved in next to Clint.

"Clint," I whispered, but he didn't move. I repeated his name a little louder and he opened his eyes.

"What is it?" he yawned.

"Brad's not been in bed last night. Do you know where he is?"

He opened his eyes properly and looked around and saw that in fact there were only the two of us in the bed.

"Well, I don't know where he is," Clint replied. "Don't worry, he's a big boy and will be able to look after himself."

I thought to myself that yes, he was a big boy, but I wasn't so sure that he could look after himself, and it wasn't like Brad not to say where he was going.

I went to the cupboard and pulled out my Speedo swimming costume, which I slipped on. Clint lay back on the bed and smiled at me.

"You know, you look so sexy when you wear that costume, it almost turns me on."

"What do you mean almost? It should turn you on completely, but enough of this messing about, what are you planning on doing today?"

"I haven't actually thought about it," he said, looking as though his mind had gone into the distance.

"Why don't we go the beach for some more fun," I said. "We can always leave a message here for Brad and when he comes back, he can join us on the beach if he likes."

"OK, I don't have a problem with that," replied Clint, hauling himself from the bed and stretching in front of the window. When he had finished stretching and turned towards me, I could see that huge cock of his swaying in the air looking like a snake that's rearing its head, and getting ready to spit.

"Put that thing away," I joked, "it's far too dangerous to have it loose around here."

Just as Clint was pulling on a pair of shorts, there was a knock on the door and Vasilis came into the room.

"Good morning, did you sleep well, my beauties?" he asked.

"Yes thanks," I answered.

"Where's Brad," he asked, and Clint and I looked at each other.

"We thought that you might be able to tell us," replied Clint. "Joe thought Brad might have spent the night with you."

"I haven't seen him since he apparently left for Delos, yesterday," said Vasilis, looking worried. "If he didn't return from Delos, then I'm very worried."

"Are you sure that he went to Delos?" I asked.

"Yes, he apparently told my mother he was going when he got up in the morning."

"But why would you be so worried?" I asked.

"Remember I told you it was the place of Apollo," continued Vasilis, "and to be careful?"

"Yes, I remember," I said, "but what are you getting at?"

"If he has met with Apollo, who knows what might happen," said Vasilis.

"Oh come on, Vasilis, Apollo was a mythical character; how can Brad meet him?"

"There is apparently a giant of a man called Apollo who stays on the island. He works there. I have heard stories about him, but I have never met or seen him," said Vasilis.

"Oh, you mean Brad might have met this giant and fallen for him and spent the night having sex with him," I stated, laughing as I said it. "Well if that is the case, I'm sure that Brad would be only too happy."

"No, I'm serious," said Vasilis. "Some of the stories I have heard are not good."

From the expression on his face, I could see that he really meant it, and that he was not joking.

"So, if he is with this 'giant', what do we do?" asked Clint, who had been listening intently to us.

"We go to Delos and look for him," said Vasilis. "I'll go with you and help to find him."

And so it was decided that we would head to Delos in search of Brad, assuming that he was still on the island.

While we prepared to catch a boat to Delos to look for Brad, Brad had woken up in the room on Delos. He opened his eyes and looked around. He was lying on the hard bed and the only light that entered the room came from a relatively small window with some thin bars over the opening. He was alone in the room. He thought he must have overslept and that Apollo had already gone to work. He rose from the bed and crossed to the door. He tried to open it, but it was locked from the outside. He looked out of the window and shouted, but nothing materialized from his call. He went back to the bed and sat down, thinking about his situation. He remembered what Vasilis had said about being careful on the island, and realized that he had been trapped.

Brad began to feel hungry and wanted something to drink. He remembered that Apollo had splashed water on him the night before, so he went over to the bucket and drank some of the water. He went back to the bed and lay down on the hard board. He must have dozed off to sleep for a while, because when he awoke again,

Apollo was in the room with him. When he saw Apollo, he jumped from the bed and said, "Why did you lock me in?"

"I didn't want you to leave," he said. "Are you hungry?"

"Yes," I replied.

"Yes, Master," said Apollo.

"To hell with this master business," said Brad angrily.

Immediately, Apollo slapped him across the face.

"I'm sorry," said Apollo, "I didn't mean to do that, but you need to obey."

Brad stared at him in shock, but didn't say a word. No one had ever slapped him like that before and to receive such a slap was foreign to him. He wondered what Clint and Joe were doing. Were they worried about him and would they come looking for him, he wondered? He began to feel vulnerable here under Apollo's control.

"I'll get you something to eat," said Apollo, as he left the room, locking the door behind him. He wasn't gone for very long when he returned with a plate of food and something to drink. He handed it to Brad who took it and guzzled the food down. He drank the drink that was given to him, but at the time he thought it tasted odd.

"What sort of drink is this?" he asked Apollo.

"It's an herbal drink that we make on the island," was the reply.

Before Brad was able to finish the drink, he began to have a strange feeling. He was aware of everything around him and what was happening, but he felt that he was unable to do anything about it or prevent things from happening. He felt detached and disconnected to things around him and he felt almost as though he had been anesthetized

Apollo asked him how he felt, and Brad replied that he felt light-headed.

"Why don't you lie down?" said Apollo, helping Brad to lie on the bed.

Once he had got Brad lying down, he slipped out of his clothes and lay on the bed next to Brad, who was still naked from the night before. He ran his hands over Brad's chest.

"You are so smooth," Apollo said, soothingly.

His hands moved down towards Brad's cock and he wrapped them around it and started squeezing it to get it hard. As hard as Brad tried not to get a hard-on, his brain was not listening to him. Slowly Apollo could feel Brad getting harder. He then moved down to take Brad's cock in his mouth and started moving his mouth up and down the length of Brad's erect cock. Brad just lay there unable to prevent the treatment he was getting. This continued for some time until Apollo slipped from Brad, got off the bed and rolled Brad over on to his stomach. Apollo pulled Brad's ass-cheeks apart and started licking in between them. His tongue moved in and out of Brad's asshole, and Brad could feel a wonderful sensation, but under the circumstances, he didn't want this to happen, but was unable to prevent it.

Apollo once again got off the bed and found a condom which he slipped onto his thick cock and went back to making Brad's asshole wet. He then went between Brad's legs and, holding on to Brad's hips, pulled his ass into the air so that Brad was being supported by his knees and his shoulders and head on the bed.

Apollo positioned the bulbous head of his cock at Brad's entry passage, and, holding onto Brad's hips, he pushed forward and entered Brad. Brad never made a sound.

Once Apollo had entered him, he started pumping his cock in and out of Brad's ass. All that could be heard was Apollo's grunting as he forced his way in and out of Brad, and the sound of his balls slapping against Brad's butt as he entered him. He kept up this pounding for some time until Apollo could feel himself ready to offload into Brad. His pace quickened and Brad's body jolted backwards and forwards as Apollo reached his climax. With a guttural growl, Apollo shot his load into Brad and kept pumping for some time. When he had emptied himself in Brad, he pulled his cock out, removed the condom and went and lit a marijuana cigarette. Brad simply slid his stomach onto the bed and lay there.

While all this had been going on, Clint, Vasilis and I had landed on Delos and were in the process of trying to find Brad. Vasilis had managed to find someone who worked on the island and asked this person where we might find Apollo and exactly what he looked like. Having been told where he was excavating, we headed off towards the area.

"I don't think we should make our presence known to him," suggested Clint, "because we don't know where Brad is and we don't want Apollo to become suspicious."

As we neared the area where he was supposed to be working, we saw someone else who looked as though they might be employed on the island. We asked this person where Apollo was. The elderly man said that Apollo had gone home, yet in telling us this, he seemed anxious, and that worried us.

"Where is his home?" asked Vasilis, in Greek.

The man pointed in a particular direction and said something to Vasilis in Greek.

"What did he say, Vasilis?" asked Clint.

"He said we must be careful because Apollo has not been seen for some time and when that happens, it's because he's drugged up."

Both Clint and I looked at each other for support, because we were unaware of what might lie ahead of us.

"Come, guys," said Vasilis, heading off in the direction he had been shown. "Keep your eyes open for him," said Vasilis, and we both followed him.

The terrain was no better than that of Mykonos. It was rugged and barren. There was not a tree in sight and the heat hit us even though we had thought we were becoming used to the island heat. The sweat was pouring down our faces, necks and arms, yet we kept heading in the direction we'd been told.

It was later in the afternoon when we saw a building set away from all other buildings. We approached with caution. The house was set among some rocks, although most of the island was barren. We could see some smoke coming from a chimney as we approached, cautiously.

"I'll kill him if he's hurt Brad," said Clint angrily.

"Just relax, Clint. We're not going to barge in and beat anyone up. For all we know, Brad might be enjoying this guy's company," I said, realizing that Clint obviously cared very much for Brad.

I couldn't have been more wrong.

We neared the house quietly. The front door was closed so we wandered around the house and saw a window in one of the walls with thin bars over it. We crept up to the window and as I was taller than the other two, I said that I would look through the window and see if there was anything inside. I gingerly raised my head to the window. As I got closer to it, I could hear muffled noises coming from the room. I peeped through the window and saw Brad lying in the sling hanging from the roof. His legs were in the air, tied to the chains, but his arms hung limply over the edge of the sling. This huge 'giant' of a man stood between Brad's legs with his cock embedded in Brad's asshole, pounding at Brad. I watched dumbstruck. I could see that Brad seemed to be drugged, but tears were running down his cheeks. The 'giant' also seemed to be in a trance and was fucking Brad as though he were a machine. There were no feelings in this sexual act; it was pure animalistic lust. I lowered my head to where Clint and Vasilis were. The look on my face must have said a great deal.

"What did you see?" asked Clint.

"Oh Clint, he's hurting," I said, quietly.

"What do you mean, 'he's hurting'"? Asked Clint angrily.

I held him by the arm and said, "This Apollo is busy fucking Brad, who looks drugged to me, but we need to make a plan."

This news made Clint even angrier. "I'll kill him," he hissed.

"Perhaps we should wait until it's dark and then break in," suggested Vasilis.

"I need to see," said Clint. "Joe, kneel on the ground and let me stand on your back so that I can look through the window."

I obliged and knelt on the ground. Clint climbed onto my back and peered through the barred window,

The muscular Apollo, in his drugged state, was still pounding Brad's ass. Clint could see that Apollo was drugged on something and he knew that in this state, Apollo could keep fucking Brad for hours before he would come. He could also see that Brad seemed drugged. Something had to be done. He climbed off my back and headed round the house to the front door. He bashed on the door but no-one answered it. He then tried to smash down the door, but it wouldn't break. Vasilis rushed around to Clint and tried to calm him down.

"Wait until it's dark," said Vasilis, "I have a plan that we could break the bars on the window, get in and get Brad out again."

"But darkness will still be hours away," said Clint, panic in his voice. "I can't wait here to see him fucking Brad like that. He's going to split the poor guy if he carries on like that."

Both Vasilis and I tried to calm Clint down as best we could and so we remained under the barred window, hearing the grunts and groans of the two men in the small room.

We waited until it was dark, which took hours, sitting on the ground under Brad's window, contemplating what we might do to rescue Brad. The grunting and muffled sounds had stopped some time back and when I looked through the window, I could see Brad lying naked on the wooden bed, but I couldn't see Apollo. I called through the window to Brad.

"Brad, are you awake?" I called softly.

There was a groan from inside the room.

"Who's that?" came Brad's soft, disquieted reply.

"It's Clint, Vasilis and me," I said, "and we've come to rescue you. Are you alone in the room?"

Brad staggered as best he could towards the window and put his hand through the opening. I grabbed his hand and squeezed it. "Hang in, kid, we'll get you out."

"Be careful," said Brad, "he's in the room next door, but I think he's still drugged up from his marijuana."

Clint then came to the window and made Vasilis kneel on the ground so that he could look through.

"Brad, I want you to push the bars from the inside while I pull from the outside," said Clint. "Hopefully, we might get them to snap and get you out this way."

Brad and Clint started pushing and pulling at the metal bars. Although the bars began to bend, they didn't snap. This continued for some time, but we could see that this was not the way to get in. Brad then came up with an idea.

"I'll call him and say that I need the toilet. He'll have to unlock the door and then perhaps I'll be able to unlock the front door, in which case you can come in."

We all agreed that it was worth a try.

Brad went back to his bed and shouted, "Apollo, I need the toilet."

There was no response, so Brad tried again. "Apollo, are you there? I need to go to the toilet."

Brad waited a while and then he heard Apollo's footsteps.

"He's coming," Brad whispered to us at the window. We ran round to the front door to wait and see if we could get in.

Apollo unlocked Brad's door to let him out.

"What's the problem?" asked the drowsy Apollo.

"I need the toilet," replied Brad.

"I think I also need the toilet," said Apollo.

Suddenly Brad had an idea. "Well, while I'm using the toilet," he said, "you can go outside and water the plants."

He hoped that Apollo would open the front door and go out, allowing Clint and the rest of us to get in. This is precisely what happened.

Apollo opened the front door and walked a little way from the house. We could see from the light coming from the house that he was naked with his fat cock swinging from side to side as he walked. Clint, Vasilis and I rushed into the house to find Brad. We found him back in his room, standing in a corner, waiting for us.

Clint suddenly took charge and said, "I'm not leaving until I've sorted that guy out."

"We're not going to have a fight are we?" I asked.

"No way," said Clint, "I'm going to give him a taste of his own medicine."

"Let's just get Brad out of here," I insisted, not wanting to wait around for the giant to return.

"No way!" said Clint sternly. "This guy needs to be dealt with."

"But what if he finds us and locks us in? Then we've had it; we'll never get out."

"Joe, I'm not leaving until I've dealt with him."

We all stood in Brad's room, waiting for Apollo to return. When he did, he sauntered into Brad's room and was very surprised to see three other people in the room with Brad.

"Who are you?" Apollo asked staring blankly at us, not quite knowing where we had come from.

"We're going to be your worst nightmare," said Clint advancing towards Apollo. "I believe you like to hit people and fuck them and make them grovel?"

"I don't know what you're talking about," responded Apollo, arrogantly.

"Grab him," shouted Clint; and Vasilis, Brad and I grabbed Apollo.

"Tie him to that rack," shouted Clint.

Although Apollo made an effort to resist, and struggled fiercely, we struggled with him until we had him under control and we did as we were told. While we tied him to the rack, Clint selected a cane that had been lying among the whips.

"Let's see if you like this," he said, and proceeded to hit Apollo across the ass. Apollo shouted out in pain, but the more he shouted, the more Clint hit him.

"Do you like this?" asked Clint.

"No!" exclaimed Apollo.

"No, Master," shouted Clint.

"No master," said a suddenly subdued Apollo.

Clint continued this for a little while and then said, "Untie him and put him in the sling, I think that I'm ready for him."

We untied Apollo and turned him round to drag him to the sling. As we did so, we all saw how his cock had developed a full erection from the beating and a little pre-cum was dribbling from his cock.

When I saw this, it immediately aroused me.

We tied his hands to the chains of the sling, and lifted his legs into the air. Brad moved over to where Apollo had put the dildo that he had used on him and picked it up and advanced on Apollo. Apollo saw what Brad had in his hand and appealed to him not to use it. It was amazing how pathetic this giant of a man was becoming.

"Why not?" questioned Clint, "it could be quite nice."

Brad took the dildo and placed it at Apollo's asshole.

"Feel what it's like," said Brad pushing the dildo deep into Apollo.

Apollo tensed, but Brad kept pushing, then he started sliding it in and out of Apollo's ass. With the dildo rubbing Apollo's prostate, he was in ecstasy, knowing that he would soon shoot his load if they carried on.

"Don't," he appealed, "or I'll come."

"We can't have that yet," said Clint.

Brad pulled the dildo out until the head was just inside Apollo's ass. He moved it in and out in quick movements. While he did this, Clint stripped out of his clothes, put a condom onto his huge cock and stood between Apollo's legs with his ten–inch, hard cock waiting to slide it into Apollo's ass.

"What do you think of that?" I asked, holding Apollo's head up so that he could see Clint's huge cock.

There was a look of shock in his face, because he realized that it was very much bigger than his own.

Clint aimed his cock at Apollo's asshole and pushed. Apollo tried to prevent entry, but Clint was not going to give in. He kept pushing forward until he felt his cock break through Apollo's ass muscles. He entered, gasped and felt the warmth of Apollo's ass.

Immediately Apollo screamed from the pain and his ass muscles clamped around Clint's cock. Clint gave another deep sigh because this was probably the tightest ass that he had ever entered. Clint was so surprised by the tightness that he slowly pushed deeper into Apollo. Although he didn't really care what Apollo felt, but as far as he was concerned, this was a good ass to fuck. He held onto Apollo's legs attached to the chains and started swinging the sling towards and away from him. As he did so, he found that he didn't have to do much movement, because the sling was causing his cock to go really deep into Apollo and then nearly pop out. This deep movement into Apollo's tight ass was turning Clint on and his breathing was becoming heavier. Clint was surprisingly enjoying the fuck. We had also been turned on watching Clint sliding in and out of Apollo, and had all stripped off our clothes.

Vasilis and I stood on either side of Apollo, stroking our hard cocks while Brad stood behind Apollo and put his nine-inch dick into Apollo's mouth. With the movement of the sling, Brad's cock slid in an out of Apollo's mouth. Vasilis stopped playing with his cock and bent over Apollo's cock and took its fatness into his mouth. I could see that Vasilis was really enjoying this. He salivated all over Apollo's cock, making it wet and slippery. I bent over from the other side and joined him, our tongues and mouths running up and down Apollo's thick cock. Vasilis moved away from the sling and went in search of a condom, which he found and unrolled onto Apollo's cock. I wondered what he had in mind, but I didn't have to wait long. While Clint was pounding Apollo's ass and Apollo was sucking Brad off, Vasilis climbed onto the sling and sat astride Apollo's midriff. He held Apollo's cock erect and slowly lowered himself onto it. He wriggled his ass on Apollo's cock and could feel it deep inside of him. Clint, in the meantime, had motioned for me to take over from him, fucking Apollo. He pulled his cock out, got a clean condom and walked round to behind Brad who was still busy being sucked. As he left, I pulled on a condom and slipped into Apollo's ass. This guy had obviously never been fucked before because his ass was definitely one of the tightest I had ever had wrapped around my cock. Clint put his arms around Brad and gently slipped into him. The way he did it almost said that Brad no longer had to worry about anything.

Vasilis was bouncing up and down on Apollo's cock like someone riding in a rodeo, when he suddenly let out a shout and started shooting his cum over Apollo's chest. When he had finished coming, he didn't get off Apollo, but carried on riding his cock. Apollo was getting closer to coming because his breathing became much heavier. With me fucking him, Vasilis riding his cock and

Apollo sucking off Brad, we all knew that Apollo would have to blow his load soon.

I knew that it was happening when he let go of Brad's cock and shouted, "I'm coming! Oh fuck, I'm going to shoot! Fuck me! Fuck me deeper!"

I pumped his ass furiously so that my balls slapped loudly against his ass. I grabbed his legs and tried to pull him further onto my cock. I wanted to get my balls inside his tight ass as well.

"Oh Fuck!" I shouted and sent one load after another into his hot ass.

This frantic movement caused Apollo's mouth to go back onto Brad's cock, but Brad pulled away. When I had exhausted my supply of cum, I pulled my limp cock from Apollo and moved away from between his legs. As I did so, Clint pulled out of Brad and the two of them moved to between Apollo's legs. Brad slid a condom onto his cock and slipped it into Apollo's ass which was well lubricated from sweat and spit. When he had entered Apollo, Clint slid his monster barge pole back into Brad. As Clint fucked Brad, so the movement caused Brad's cock to slide deep into Apollo. Vasilis and I took up position on either side of Apollo's face and took it in turns to push our cocks into his waiting mouth, urging him to get us to cum again.

Vasilis, like the rest of us, was incredibly horny and said to me, "Joe, won't you fuck me?"

I obliged by turning Apollo's face towards Vasilis so that Vasilis' cock could slide in and out of Apollo's mouth. I went behind Vasilis, held him around the waist and slowly slid my dick into him. I could feel him pushing back onto me. He wriggled his sexy ass, trying to get me deeper into him. I wanted to be gentle with him, but he turned to me and said, "Fuck me hard, Joe. I want to feel you deep inside of me."

I did as I was told and pounded into his ass. The more I pounded, the more he pushed onto my cock, wriggling his ass. Brad watched this as he was fucking Apollo. This must have turned him on because I noticed how he increased his rhythm and never took his eyes off Vasilis.

"I'm going to shoot," shouted Vasilis.

He pulled his cock from Apollo's mouth and showered a spray of cum onto Apollo's face. He kept shooting and as he did so, his ass muscles tightened around my cock. I increased my speed and he bent over, almost in an effort to get me deeper into him.

"Aaargh!" I grunted and let fly into Vasilis.

I pushed hard into him causing him to fall forward onto Apollo and felt my body shaking from the excitement. Brad leant across Apollo and grabbed Vasilis' nipples and squeezed.

He gave one final deep push into Apollo and sighed, "I'm going to come; I'm going to come."

"Come baby," said Clint holding onto Brad's shoulders and forcing his pile driver deep into his friend.

They both let out groans of ecstasy as they fired their loads into the waiting asses. Brad put his hands behind his back to pull Clint deeper into him. He slid his cock from Apollo, but held onto Clint.

"Don't pull out," he appealed to Clint. "It's so good when you're inside me." Clint stood there with his arms wrapped around Brad, gently stroking Brad's nipples and knowing that Brad was now safe.

Eventually, Clint slipped gently from Brad and they stood there and kissed each other.

While Vasilis and I tried to clean ourselves, Apollo lay exhausted in the sling. Clint moved to Apollo, his huge cock now hanging limply between his legs, looked at him and said, "Did you like what you got?"

Apollo didn't know what to say, but from the expression on his face, I think he enjoyed what he had got. In fact, he probably assumed the role of master simply because of the size of his body and felt that because he was so big, no one could fuck him, but he didn't reckon on Clint! As we sat in the room, I gave it some thought and realized that apart from Vasilis, who I don't think would ever fuck anybody; Clint was the only one of us who had not fucked Apollo and left their load inside him.

As we could not return to Mykonos until daylight the next day, Apollo was obliged to let us stay the night in his home. He obviously felt bad about what had happened to Brad because he offered his own bed to Brad and whoever else wanted to share it and said that he would sleep on the wooden bed in the sling room. We couldn't all fit into his bed, so Vasilis and I said that Brad and Clint could use it. The two went off to the main room, leaving Vasilis, Apollo and I to sleep in the sling room. Vasilis and I climbed onto the wooden bed while Apollo lay in the sling, saying that he was quite happy to spend the night there.

However, before we all fell asleep, Clint locked the cottage front door and took the key with him, so that Apollo couldn't escape during the night.

We dozed off to sleep with Vasilis curled up next to me, and it must have been in the early hours of the morning that I heard a slight squeaking noise accompanied by audible breathing. I wondered if Brad and Clint were at it in Apollo's bed, but the noise seemed to be closer.

I lay and listened; then I heard Clint say. "I started something, but I never finished it."

I suddenly realized that it was the sling that was making the squeaking sound, but who was in it?

"Do you like my cock inside of you?" I heard Clint say.

"Yes", came the reply and I realized it was Apollo.

"Do you want me to fuck you deep and hard?"

"Oh yes please," came Apollo's reply.

Even in the dark I could visualize this giant of a man, lying there being fucked by Clint. My cock started to get hard. Vasilis snuggled a little closer causing my cock to rub against his ass.

"Push it right in," said Apollo.

I pushed a little harder against Vasilis' ass. This time he met my push and pushed back. I knew he wasn't asleep. The sound of the squeaking sling became more pronounced and their grunts became louder.

"Oh fuck me! Fuck me harder!" exclaimed Apollo not worrying now whether he said it out aloud. "I want you to shoot your load inside me; come all over me."

I could hear Clint really pounding hard into Apollo. Clint's balls were slapping against Apollo's ass and I moved my cock and balls closer to Vasilis' entry passage.

I heard Clint say, "Fuck, but you've got a nice tight ass. You grip my cock like a vice."

"Do you like that feeling?" asked Apollo.

"Yes. I want you to milk my cock dry when I come."

I felt Vasilis place his hand on my cock and guide it into his ass. He pushed slowly onto it and gave out a sigh as it sank into him. I let him do most of the initial work so that I didn't hurt him as I made my entry.

He pushed right onto me and I felt the full length of my dick sink into him. "Oh yes", he groaned and I started rhythmically moving in and out of him.

As I did so, I whispered in his ear, "Will you milk my cock dry when I come?"

"Of course," came the reply.

As our movements increased, so the wooden bed made some noises causing Clint and Apollo to freeze for a moment. They could obviously hear our rapid breathing and realized what we were doing, so they continued where they had left off.

I knew Clint well and I knew when he was getting close from the sound of his breathing patterns and that moment was nearing. I also increased my speed because I wanted to come at the same time as they did.

Clint was now holding onto Apollo's shoulders pushing himself ever deeper into Apollo.

"I'm going to come; oh fuck, I'm going to come," I heard Clint say.

"So am I," said Apollo.

My breathing was now very heavy and I wrapped my hand around Vasilis' cock, which he had been stroking, and worked furiously on it. He gasped and I felt his warm cum run down my hand. I kept fucking him and stroking him. His warm cum made his cock slick and turned me on.

"Oh Fuuuck," I shouted and pumped everything I had in me into Vasilis' ass as he pushed harder onto my cock.

The chains from the sling were now squeaking loudly and so were the sound effects coming from Clint and Apollo as Apollo shot his hot cum over his stomach and chest.

"Fuck me! Fuck my ass. Deeper; harder; Oh yes, Fuck me!" exclaimed Apollo and Clint emptied his load in Apollo's ass.

Apollo's ass muscles tightened round Clint's cock and I heard Clint gasp, "Squeeze it hard; milk it. Oh that's so good. Oh yes!"

After Clint had withdrawn from Apollo, I heard him go into the other room and Apollo slid onto the wooden bed next to Vasilis and me.

I could feel some of my cum sliding out of Vasilis' ass as I pulled my cock out. I lay there pressing my wet cock against Vasilis' butt with my arms around him and could feel Apollo's thick wet cock pressed up hard against my butt.

We didn't get much sleep that night because I think that Apollo had found something new that day. I forget how many times I came that night, but I do know that before the sun came up the next day, I had fucked Apollo's ass twice and he had also fucked mine and Vasilis hadn't been left out either, because both Apollo and I fucked Vasilis one after another.

When the sun rose and I awoke, I laughed because I realized that my cock was in Vasilis and Apollo's was in me and that we'd slept like that during the night, connected. I rolled over, disconnecting myself from Vasilis and Apollo, and lay facing Apollo. I looked at his peaceful looking face and wondered why he had treated Brad, and possibly others, the way he had. He must have sensed that I was looking at him because he opened his eyes and smiled at me. I felt his hand search for my cock, find it and give it a squeeze. I did the same to him and smiled back at him. Maybe deep down he really wasn't a master, but perhaps a slave.

When everyone was up and about, Apollo made breakfast for us and gave a wrapped gift to Brad.

"I apologize for everything I did to you, but it was because I found you so attractive and didn't want you to go. I know that what you all did to me was because you were angry, but I think it has shown me another side to myself, and for that I'm grateful."

He hugged each of us and said that he hoped he would see us again, but when he said goodbye to Clint, he hugged him with passion and kissed him on each cheek.

"I'm grateful to you, Clint. You actually made me feel special." He turned to Brad and said, "I'm sorry, but last night Clint and I got together to finish some unfinished business."

Brad smiled at him and said, "It's OK, Apollo, I know, Clint told me."

Clint put his arm around Apollo's shoulder and laughing, said, "don't let anyone tell you that you're the biggest asshole they've met, because they would be lying; you're the tightest asshole I've ever experienced."

We all laughed, and with the exception of Vasilis, we all agreed with Clint because we'd all been there and felt it.

"To you, Vasilis," said Apollo, "now that you've met me and you know what I'm like; anytime you're in this part of the world or you just feel you need some pleasure, you know where I am."

"You bet," replied Vasilis, "in fact, can I book you for next week?"

"What day?" joked Apollo.

"The whole week," laughed Vasilis

Apollo saw us down to the harbor and onto the boat, and then set off to carry on excavating ruins. As we sailed away from Delos, I wondered if we would ever see him again and whether we had changed his entire sex life. Brad and Clint sat on the boat engrossed in each other's conversation, while Vasilis seemed to be deep in thought. Perhaps he was already thinking about next week. When we reached Mykonos harbor, I knew something exciting had happened in our lives; something that didn't start off well, but which had ended on a high and I wondered if there would be anything to top it.

We got back to Vasilis' house and all immediately went to sleep to make up for the lack of sleep, but before doing so, we all agreed that there would be no sex until at least the next day.

CHAPTER 8

THE RETURN TO APOLLO

We slept the rest of that day and night and woke up the next day refreshed. Brad unwrapped his present from Apollo, to find a beautiful statue of the mythical god, Apollo, probably as a reminder of his experience on Delos.

"How are you feeling, Brad?" asked Clint when he awoke.

"I'm fine thanks. It was a frightening experience, but I think I'm over it now. It was weird when I was 'drugged'. I don't know what he gave me but I seemed to have no control over myself and I wasn't able to stop him from doing whatever he wanted to me."

"It was probably K," replied Clint.

"What's that?" I enquired.

"It's a drug that often lands up in people's drinks and they become almost unable to feel any pain and become immune to whatever's happening to them," said Clint.

We dressed and ate breakfast, after which we packed a bag of water and fruit and Clint, Brad and I set off for the beach.

We caught the rickety bus and went as far as Platys Yalos, but didn't catch a boat to the adjoining beaches; instead we chose to walk across the rugged countryside until we came upon a deserted cove. We inched our way down the cliff path and found ourselves on a small stretch of white sand and a clear blue sea, lapping the shore. We put down our towels and undressed. Clothing on some of Greece's beaches is optional, and we chose to take everything off. We lay there feeling the hot sun beat down onto our bodies. Nobody had made mention of the previous night's events on Delos, until I spoke up and said, "What do you think of Apollo, Clint?"

There was a moment of silence as Clint was thinking, and then he said, "I actually find him quite sexy, if you forget what he did to Brad."

We never reacted vocally, but I thought to myself that he was quite right.

"He's also got the tightest ass I've ever been into," continued Clint.

"What about mine" piped up Brad?

"Yours is not tight; it's just hot!" explained Clint. "Well, you fucked him, what did you think, Brad?"

"I suppose you're right," he said, "he's actually got a nice ass, but I also think he's incredibly good looking."

"I'll second that," I said, "and I know Vasilis thinks he's the greatest."

I lay there thinking for a while then I said, "Do you realize that each one of us is attracted to him for some reason or another; that in fact, although we wanted him to endure pain for what he had done to Brad, each one of us, Apollo included, endured pleasure."

There was silence as this sank in and they thought about it.

"You mean that we're almost like his slaves? That each of us wants him for a certain reason; that we are almost worshipping him?" asked Clint.

"Yes," I replied, "I suppose you could say that. You, Clint would probably want him for his tight ass; Brad would want him for his looks; I would want him for his looks, ass and cock, although I prefer yours and Clint's," I said jabbing Brad in the side as we lay on the sand, "and Vasilis would just want to be fucked by him."

At that, we all laughed and Brad jumped up from his towel and said, "Come on you horny devils, let's go for a swim," and raced towards the water's edge.

Clint and I followed and the three of us frolicked in the calm sea, splashing each other, laughing and just enjoying living and the fact that we had Brad back with us.

"I wonder what he would have done to you if we hadn't arrived there to rescue you, Brad?" asked Clint.

"I dread to think."

"Thank goodness you told Vasilis's mother that you were going to Delos, otherwise we might never have found you," I added.

After a steaming hot day at the beach and a cooling rest in the afternoon in the confines of the whitewashed room, we showered and readied ourselves for a fun evening of eating, clubbing and dancing.

Vasilis had a prior engagement with his mother to visit some family members, so he wouldn't be able to accompany us on our evening's outing, but we had enquired from him how to get to some of the clubs and bars, as we were well aware of how easy it was to get lost in the lanes around Mykonos.

Vasilis had told us of a wonderful little bar which catered for sundowners and which he said was very romantic with a pleasant crowd of people. Although it was 8.00pm, the sun was still blazing down. This was typically a Greek summer; the only consolation was that the Meltemi wind, a summer wind, was blowing and cooling the air.

We arrived at this quaint bar, set on the water's edge. On entering, we were not sure whether this was someone's private home or not as the seating area was made up of couches, easy chairs, large scatter cushions, original paintings done by the locals and classical music, playing in the background.

There were already a few people sitting around chatting, so we found space for ourselves and ordered the drinks of the house, daiquiris. The setting was absolutely superb. A large window opened up over the sea and a cool sea breeze filtered in. The music quietly fitted into the background and the people there were very friendly.

While we were sitting enjoying the atmosphere, Brad and I noticed a fish come up from the sea and go past the window. We both leapt from where we were sitting and rushed to the window. Were fish jumping out of the sea? No! There above us, as we peered out of the window, was a young boy with a piece of fishing nylon in his hand and he had just caught this fish which we had seen. Presumably, this was dinner for the night.

After spending about an hour drinking daiquiris, we made our way to our own dinner, after which we had decided to head for the bars and clubs.

By midnight, we had arrived at a club where a number of both sexes were enjoying themselves to the latest sounds. We paid and went in, buying some drinks as we did so. The vibe was very festive with everyone enjoying themselves. These were the so-called beautiful people, and among them there were some really beautiful people. As a result of the heat and the limited space in the club, most of the guys were topless, making viewing a pleasure. There was so much talent to choose from that poor Brad was becoming frustrated, because no sooner had he seen one good looking guy, then another hunk would appear and he would lose interest in the previous guy, and so this went on all night.

At about 1.30am a drag artist appeared to much whistling and cheering and proceeded to keep the clients entertained for about twenty minutes.

By 2.30am, we were all feeling a little exhausted, so Brad said that he was heading home, but Clint and I, although tired, were not ready for bed so while Brad made his way home, we made our way to the harbor area for some early morning coffee.

We found a small taverna still open and sat in the cool night air watching the boats bobbing in the harbor with the lights dancing on the water's surface. The harbor area was quite active with people still eating and drinking while others spent a romantic evening together.

Once we had finished our coffee, Clint and I wandered around the area until I spotted a tall, slim, good looking guy. I decided to make a move on the guy and started chatting to him. I found out that he too was on holiday from Germany and his name was Helmut. We chatted for a while with Clint choosing to keep his distance, and then Helmut and I set off in the direction of a nearby church. Clint followed, both keeping an eye on me and hoping to see what we were up to.

Helmut and I went behind the small church and started kissing. Our lips devoured each other and in our ecstasy, our shirts were pulled off and flung to the ground. Although slim, he had a beautifully chiseled chest that tapered down to a small waist.

My lips moved to the rotund nipples, savoring their taste and nibbling gently at them. Both of us had a hard-on by this stage and our hands searched each other's body until each of us found the other's pleasure maker.

Through the soft material of his pants I could feel the long, hard rod, waiting to be released from its confines. I found the zip, pulled it down and inserted my hand to take hold of his cock. It felt thick as I held it and started sliding my hand along its length. At about the same time, he ventured into my jeans and extracted my cock. Immediately, he sank to his knees and took my cock into his warm mouth.

I felt the tightness of his lips as he slid his mouth from the tip to the base, and I thrust forward, almost gagging him. I then put my hands under his armpits and lifted him where our mouths met once more.

I went back to working on his nipples and then ran my tongue down his chest, over his taut stomach to wrap my mouth around his fat cock- head. Helmut groaned quietly as I lubricated his cock-head with my tongue. His cock resembled a mushroom with a long, streamlined stem and a large bulbous head.

He put a hand into his pants' pocket and produced a condom pack which he tore open and then handed the condom to me, in order that I might roll it down his length. Once I had done that, I undid his pants, letting them and his briefs fall to his ankles. I stood up and undid my jeans, shucking them and my briefs to the ground.

Gently, Helmut turned me around so that I was now facing the church wall. He spread my legs then knelt down to rim my ass in preparation for his assault.

Once I was sufficiently lubricated, he stood up, held the long stem of his cock and aimed for my hole. I felt the bulbous head forcing its way into my chute. I rested my hands against the church wall for support as Helmut slowly pushed forward. I felt the huge head break through and gain entry. I can only describe the feeling as one of sheer bliss. His tightness in my ass made me ecstatic to the extent that at one stage I thought I was going to faint, the feeling was so intense. I'd had my fair share of men, but none had created such a feeling before. His bulbous head rubbed against my prostate, driving me into a state of delirium, and as he slowly drove in and out, I could feel my chute being opened up as his cock-head expanded.

He was uncannily slow in his movements – so unlike so many others who simply pound you to death. My groans were growing decidedly louder with each gentle thrust. He was midway to pushing deeper, when he suddenly froze and stopped. I turned my head to see why there had been the sudden halt, and in the available light from the nearby street light, I saw Clint standing behind Helmut.

Clint's crotch was rubbing up against Helmut's naked ass and he was rubbing it over Helmut's bubble-butt crack. Helmut removed a hand from my shoulder, where he'd been holding me, and I felt him put his arm around Clint and pull him closer. I felt myself being pushed up closer to the church wall.

Helmut unzipped Clint's jeans and pulled out his weapon, which Helmut began to stroke. Clint dug into his pocket and pulled out a condom which he unrolled onto his throbbing cock, and then he bent down and salivated over Helmut's asshole, while the German continued to service me.

Clint stood up and, guiding his hard rod, entered Helmut. A sigh emitted from both Clint and Helmut as the warmth of Helmut's ass encompassed Clint's cock. The three of us were now attached and began to work as a team. Helmut was sandwiched between Clint and me, so was being service at both ends. The unison and harmony between the three of us in our thrusts was an incredible feeling. The deeper that Clint pushed into Helmut, the deeper his swollen cock-head sank into me.

My body began to shudder as I neared my climax.

"I'm going to come," I gasped, even though no-one had touched my cock.

Helmut immediately took hold of my cock and speeded up his thrusts, stroking me as he did so. A gasp and grunt came from deep down within me and I shot a stream of white cum which hit the white church wall and began to trickle down the wall. Another big stream followed, and another; then smaller shots covered Helmut's hand.

Clint, realizing what was happening increased his thrusts and Helmut tightened his ass muscles around Clint's cock. Both Clint and I felt Helmut's body tense and I felt his cock expand as he fired his load into my guts. At almost the same time, Clint let fly, thrusting uncontrollably, forcing me against the wall and feeling the wetness of my own cum rubbing across my stomach.

As our bodies returned to a state of normality, Clint pulled out of Helmut, who remained embedded in my chute. Slowly Helmut began to pull out of me but the feeling I experienced as his huge mushroom-shaped cock-head broke through my sphincter, almost gave me another climax the feeling was so intense.

We tried as best we could to clean ourselves, get dressed, and the three of us headed back to the harbor area and the crowds still wandering about. We went back to the taverna and ordered some drinks and spent the next hour talking and planning to meet at the beach the next day.

After finishing our drinks, Clint and I headed back home, while Helmut went his way.

When we arrived back home and before we entered, Clint and I stopped and stood under the starry sky.

"You know, Joe, although we've had fun tonight, I can't get Apollo out of my mind. It's as though I've been brain-washed or drugged or something like that – you know like a spell's been cast over me."

I smiled in the starry light. I knew exactly what Clint meant and I felt sure that if we were to ask Brad about his feelings for Apollo, he'd probably say the same thing. Sure we'd had our fair share of men during our holiday, but Apollo was something different – unexplainable.

"And where does Brad fit into this?" I enquired.

"Oh, don't get me wrong when I talk about Apollo like this. I'm not about to go into a relationship with the guy, and Brad will always be a part of my life, like I'm sure he'll be a part of yours."

"I'm glad to hear that."

"No, you guys have got nothing to worry about, but I just find it so strange that I can't get that guy out of my mind."

"Maybe we need to get to bed and then you won't think about him," I said, going into the quiet house and creeping to our room where Clint and I snuggled into bed alongside Brad.

CHAPTER 9

A LEATHER RENDEZVOUS

The following day the three of us met Helmut at Super Paradise beach, and naturally Brad began to show a very keen interest in the man, especially after Clint and I had regaled him with the details of the previous night's escapades. Brad's eyes were transfixed when Helmut undressed on the beach and his huge pendulous cock came into view. In fact I've never really seen Brad so animated before in his effort to make serious contact with a man. All this was much to Clint and my entertainment, but no matter what we said to Brad, he was determined to get Helmut, although, thinking about it, Helmut was probably keen to get Brad.

By lunch time Brad was hungry, not for conventional food, but 'male food'. It was as if he couldn't contain himself any more. He stood up, shook the sand from him and declared that he was going for a walk and would Helmut like to accompany him. So brazen, we thought, but Clint and I smiled to each other, knowing full well Brad's plan. Helmut agreed, and the two of them set off up the hill and over the rocks towards the direction of the shepherd's hut.

Brad led the way with Helmut close on his heels; two naked men in the blazing sun on their travels to a secluded building in order to satisfy each other. As they neared the hut, Helmut hesitated.

"What's that?" he enquired.

"It's a shepherd's hut," replied Brad. "It's empty and it's very cool once you get inside."

They entered the stone shell and indeed Helmut was surprised at the coolness that surrounded them. No sooner were they inside, than Brad lost all control. He couldn't wait to lay his hands on Helmut's body. He grabbed him and proceeded to attack Helmut's mouth with kisses. It was all pretty rough and frenetic. Their mouths fought to gain entry to the others and their arms were grabbing furiously at each other's body. Embraced together, they sank slowly to the soft cool ground and lay entwined in each other's arms as they rolled over in chaotic passion.

Brad moved straight down to the now famous bulbous mushroom-shaped cock-head, which he devoured without hesitation. It was clear that dear Brad was hungry for 'male meat'. Helmut lay on his back groaning in pleasure as Brad's mouth ventured along Helmut's long shaft. Brad maneuvered himself so that his erection hovered over Helmut's open mouth, waiting to be consumed. As soon as Brad felt the warmth of Helmut's mouth surrounding his cock, he was in his seventh heaven.

After a while of rapturous passion, Brad lifted his head and gasped, "I'm getting close!"

"So am I," replied Helmut, becoming frenzied in his attack on Brad's cock.

The two continued their assault until both erupted together, both swallowing as fast as they could and enjoying the sweet-saltiness of each other. Helmut lay breathing heavily as Brad kissed and licked the head of Helmut's cock, making the most of their moment together. Eventually when their erections had subsided, Helmut and Brad left the coolness of the hut and descended to the beach. Both had contented grins on their faces when they reached Clint and me.

"Enjoy yourselves?" was Clint's casual comment as they sat down on the sand next to us.

"Absolutely!" was Brad's reply, as if doubting their fun could have been anything other than enjoyable. "It was absolutely fabulous," said an exalted Brad.

For the balance of the day, Brad lay content, physically and mentally, on the sand tanning his streamline body while Clint and I splashed around in the cool waters. By midday, we were sweating from the heat and chose to catch a boat back to Platys Yalos and then back to the home.

Once we reached the coolness of the house, Vasilis was excitedly waiting for us.

"I'm so glad you got back early?"

"Why?" asked Brad. "What's happened?"

"No nothing's happened, it's just that I saw an advert for a party tonight in town, and I think we must all go."

"What sort of party, Vasilis?" I asked, wondering why he was so excited.

"It's being held at the Ramrod Club tonight and starts at 9:00p.m," replied Vasilis, still like an excited schoolboy.

"OK, so what's so special about this party that makes it different from others here on the island?" enquired Clint.

"It is a masked leather party," replied Vasilis, beaming with excitement at the thought.

"Oh hell, in this heat," said Brad with a sigh.

"It could be good," said Clint, trying to pick up on Vasilis's enthusiasm. "All you need is a harness and leather jock-strap," he continued and then you won't be hot."

"I think anyone dressed like that is hot," I answered.

"Please, you know what I mean. They won't be stifling from the heat," said Clint, looking at me with disgust.

I grinned sheepishly because I meant it to be that I liked the idea.

"So where do we get leather clothes?" asked Brad, still not having bought into the idea, although he did find guys in leather sexy.

"You don't have to worry about a thing. I have a friend who can help us out," remarked Vasilis, "but we must go early to his house to select what we want."

"You make it sound as though he has a factory full of leather clothing," I said, without sounding facetious.

"He does," beamed Vasilis. "He's a fashion designer."

When we heard that, we all seemed more eager now to get some clothing and head to the party.

We decided to forego our afternoon rest from the sun, and instead go with Vasilis to the designer's workshop.

When we arrived at the venue, which was his house, we were met by a large Greek man aged about forty-something. When we speak of large, we don't mean fat, but rather, bulky, perhaps in the same vein as Apollo.

"Guys, this is Konstantin, my designer friend, and these are Clint, Brad and Joe," said Vasilis, introducing everyone.

We all greeted Konstantin who kindly took us into his simple, yet luxuriously furnished home, and offered us something cool and refreshing to drink.

"Vasilis tells me you are going to the party tonight?" asked Konstantin, encouraging us to sit.

We sat down in his plus lounge and like a chorus; we all said that we were looking forward to the party. Konstantin looked each of us over and decided that fitting us with clothing was not going to be a problem for him.

"Are you going?" asked Clint.

"Naturally. Probably the whole town will be there; that is, the whole gay community, I mean. Did you have any particular ideas as to what you wanted to wear?"

We all shook our heads because we didn't know what type of clothing he had in stock.

"Come, let me show you what I have," said Konstantin, leading us from the lounge and into another room that had clothes hanging from a number of racks.

There were elegant evening dresses alongside leather jeans and chaps, between which were scattered day dresses and leather jackets. This was like a proliferation of materials that came in various shades and textures. Our mouths dropped open when we saw the collection and like school kids, we hurried to touch the garments.

"I also have attachments and accoutrements here as well," continued Konstantin, spreading his arms generously to show us the entire collection of items.

He looked at each of us and in his mind, decided what he thought would look good on each of us.

"Clint, I think this might suit you," said Konstantin, taking some chaps from the rack and walking over to a table on which lay studded jock-straps, ordinary leather jock-straps, harnesses, studded collars and leather wrist bands.

Konstantin picked up a harness and a studded jock-strap.

"Try these on," he said, handing Clint the garments.

Clint took them and we could see the puzzled look on Clint's face, not knowing where he could change.

"You can change here," said Konstantin, waving his arm to show Clint that he could change in front of us. "After all, we are all men, are we not?"

Perhaps Konstantin was keener on seeing four naked men in his studio. As Clint began to peel off his clothes, Konstantin handed Brad a pair of leather jeans, a leather waistcoat and a studded dog collar with a chain attached to it.

"Is this to prevent me from getting lost?" asked Brad, admiring the chain.

"You could say that," replied Konstantin, who was already busy finding something for me to wear.

I was handed a pair of leather shorts, but it wasn't until I tried them on that I realized they had a zip which went from the front, between my legs and up my ass.

"Wow!" I exclaimed. "If anyone unzips this they'll have access to my ass," I said, more from surprise than shock.

The others all laughed at my realization, but Konstantin was not to be deterred and handed me a harness as well. For Vasilis, he gave him a studded dog collar with a chain attached, a pair of leather shorts, without the zip all the way around, and a leather waistcoat.

Once we were all dressed, then Konstantin began checking to see how we looked. He seemed happy with his outfit distribution, but then Clint remembered something that Vasilis had said.

"Guys, there's something missing…"

"What?" asked Brad?

"Vasilis, you said it was a masked leather party, but we don't have masks."

Konstantin came to the rescue.

"Do not worry, I'll quickly run something up for you," he said, grabbing pieces of leather that were lying on the table with the accoutrements.

Quickly was certainly the word, because in no time, Konstantin had made four masks, although not elaborate, certainly served the purpose. With our selection of garments and newly sewn masks, we headed back to Vasilis's house, with strict instructions not to damage the goods and Vasilis would return them all the following day.

We thanked Konstantin and promised to see him later at the party, if we recognized him, and began preparing for the evening. We showered and readied ourselves, preening and posing in our new attire. Naturally, everyone had a turn at pulling the zipper on my shorts and trying to grab my ass once the zipper was opened.

We decided that the elite never arrive early so we arrived at the Ramrod Club at about 10:30p.m and already the place was thronging with people. There were chubby leather guys and muscular ones, leather masters and leather slaves, some in leather jock-straps and some in jeans, and then there was us. Go-go dancers in miniscule leather outfits that hugged their bodies, were dancing on the bar counter to loud, thumping music, while guests danced on any space they could find.

A great mix of people and music filled every conceivable space and there was much chatter among the guest as they tried to identify others there. Vasilis and I tried to squeeze our way onto what was supposed to be the dance floor and we were so crushed together, that it was almost impossible to dance. It was more like rubbing your body against somebody else's body in time to the music. Soon

Brad and Clint joined us and the four of us clung to each other as we did a four-way body rub!

When we managed to get a break from the music and grab a drink each, we were standing almost in the street when Vasilis noticed Konstantin's arrival with an equally tall, well-built man wearing leather chaps, a harness and a studded bulging jock-strap as well as a hood that covered his head. The only openings were for his eyes, nose and mouth. Konstantin, on the other hand, had on his own designer wear outfit of skin-tight leather jeans, a tight-fitting top which resembled a vest and a dog collar around his neck with a long chain that was attached to the harness of the accompanying man, so wherever the hooded man went, Konstantin was dragged along too.

"Aren't you going to introduce us to your friend, Konstantin?" asked Vasilis.

"You know this is a masked party and it is up to the guests to remain secretive," replied Konstantin.

We all admired Konstantin's erotic outfit, but we also admired the physique of the hooded friend.

"Do you think that's Konstantin's lover?" asked Clint, noticing the bulging pouch of the jock-strap.

"I don't think he's got a lover," answered Vasilis, "but he does get around with a number of guys. He's very popular, you know."

We watched as the hooded friend made his way to the bar counter, dragging Konstantin behind him. When they had got their drinks, they headed towards the street to get some fresh air and space. It was interesting to see that when they reached the street, the hooded friend pulled the chain, jerking Konstantin forward so he almost fell and the man then told the designer to sit at his feet. It was an intriguing scene to see this popular, well-known man groveling at the feet of this massive man, but it was obviously what he liked to do.

As the night dragged on, we tried to identify people we might have seen at the beach and around town, but it was very difficult because of the masks. Admittedly, some men removed their masks so that they could be identified, but we kept ours on all the time. At around 2:00a.m, Brad and I decided to take a walk and left Vasilis with Clint. As we left the club, we wandered along the harbor, away from the club, enjoying the fresh sea breeze that had built up. We wandered towards the end of the harbor where there was very little light from buildings and tavernas, and there, down a side street, we saw two dark figures; one on his knees with a chain attached to a collar around his neck, while the other had his jock-strap pulled down and was pushing his cock deeply into the kneeling man's mouth. Their grunts and groans from their action were not hushed and could easily have attracted others to watch. Brad and I stood motionless watching as the powerful bigger man plowed long, deep thrusts into his accomplice, then he pulled his cock from the warmth of his accomplice's mouth, pulled the chain to make the man stand up, turned him around, bent him over and thrust his cock into the man's ass.

I found myself being attracted to the action that the taller man was doing. There was a type of magnetism that drew me to him. I wanted to be on the receiving end of his huge cock. I wanted to be the one bending and receiving this weapon. I knew I was getting aroused and my cock was straining to break free by what I was watching, and I'm sure that Brad was also in the same way as me. I felt Brad's hand reach the zipper to my shorts and he'd soon opened it up and had his hand sliding along the crack of my ass, fingering my hole when he reached it. He didn't get very far, because before we could do anything, both men in the dark street let out guttural groans and obviously fired their loads.

No sooner had the bigger of the two emptied his load, then he jerked the chain once more getting his accomplice upright and both men got themselves presentable again. Brad and I hastily beat a retreat and headed back to the club, both very horny and both highly aroused by what we'd witnessed.

Back in the club we met up with Clint and Vasilis but never mentioned anything of what we'd seen, until Konstantin and his friend re-appeared.

"They've just been for a fuck," whispered Brad to Clint.

"And how would you know?" came the reply.

"Joe and I watched them."

"So who's the hooded guy?" asked Clint.

"Haven't a clue, but we watched as he fucked Konstantin in a dark street near the harbor."

"So I suppose you and Joe are now as horny as hell?" remarked Clint, jovially.

Both of us laughed at Clint's suggestion, but he was right. I knew I was and I was sure that Brad was as well. As we stood there talking, the hooded man walked over to us with Konstantin firmly attached to him.

"We're heading home, guys, so I'll see you tomorrow with the clothes," said Konstantin.

"Sure, and thanks again Konstantin, for the loan of these," said Brad and Vasilis together.

The hooded man smiled for the first time that whole night, but not at all of us; rather he smiled at Clint and Brad, then they turned and left, Konstantin being dragged along like a puppy. It was clear who was in control.

"Do you think you've got yourself a fan?" I asked Clint as the two men departed. "It was to you and Brad that the friend smiled."

"I never noticed," said Clint dismissively.

"You know who he reminded me of, his build that is…?" I asked.

"Who?" Asked Vasilis.

"Apollo. Their build seems similar, I think."

"Maybe," replied an unsure Vasilis, who seemed not to think the way I did.

"Well, whoever he is, he sure knew how to fuck, because old Konstantin was crooning like a coyote in that street."

I smiled at Brad's description and although I thought it funny, I sure as hell wouldn't have minded if it had been me crooning in the dark street.

By 3:00a.m we were all beginning to get tired, so we decided we'd had a good time and enough for one night, so we said our good-byes to people we had met at the party and headed home, to collapse into bed and sleep.

CHAPTER 10

A HOT SURPRISE

We spent the next three days going to the beaches, drinking at the bars in the evenings and generally admiring both the beautiful tourists and Greeks. We assumed that Helmut and Heinz must have returned home after their holiday. Eventually, the day before we were to return to Athens arrived. We had one day left on the island and then the next morning we were to catch the ferry back to Piraeus and then on to Athens.

We had not made any plans for the day, but had decided that we were not going to spend the day on the beach. Clint said that he was going to go for a walk and Brad said that he thought that he would do some last minute shopping; as for me, I hadn't decided. Clint and Brad went their different ways and then I strolled down to the harbor. I wandered around the harbor looking at the various yachts and fishing boats and then had a sudden thought. I looked for someone who might be working on one of the boats and when I saw a fisherman, I walked over to his boat and said, "Are there any boats going to Delos?"

"The main boat has just left," he replied, in broken English, "but if you want to go, I'll take you."

He told me how much it would cost. I paid him and off we set.

On the way to the island, I spoke to him and arranged for him to come back to Delos later in the day to pick me up and bring me back to Mykonos. Throughout the journey to Delos, I kept thinking of Apollo and wondering if he would be there or was I wasting my time.

Our little fishing boat chugged slowly across the open sea until we reached the harbor on Delos.

"You want to see the ruins on Delos?" asked the boat owner, as we chugged across the sea.

"Yes," I replied. In actual fact, I didn't want to see them, but rather Apollo, if he was on the island.

When we arrived at the small harbor on Delos, I thanked my captain and set off towards Apollo's house. There were quite a few tourists visiting the island, but I had no interest in them. After quite a walk, I reached Apollo's house to find the front door closed. Immediately I thought how stupid I was not to have looked for him at the excavation site first, but as I walked round the house to where I remembered there was the window through which we'd seen Brad, I heard a noise come from the room that Brad had been in. I stopped and listened. I heard Apollo's voice say to someone, "You want me to fuck you?"

"Yes," came the reply.

"Are you sure?" said Apollo.

"I want that fat cock-head sliding up my ass," came the reply, once again.

I slowly raised my head to the level of the window in order to peer in. When I did so, I could not believe what I saw.

Apollo was standing naked, his muscular legs spread apart, with his cock greased and ready to attack a waiting ass that faced him from the sling hanging in the middle of the room. I saw the sling occupant's legs hoisted in the air and attached to the chains and my eyes moved up the body and stopped as they fell on this huge throbbing dick. After I had taken that in, I continued working my view up this body until I came to the face – it was Clint. Clint was strapped into the sling and Apollo was about to fuck him. What made this all the more unbelievable was that in all the time I had known Clint, no-one had ever fucked him; he had always done it to them.

I watched as Apollo placed his swollen cock-head at the entrance to Clint's ass and slowly begin to insert it. Clint grimaced and shouted, "Oh fuck!' as Apollo sank slowly into his warm chute.

"Do you want me to take it out?" asked Apollo.

"No," Clint grunted, "just keep pushing it in."

Apollo did as he was asked, but preceded slowly so that Clint could get used to the feeling. As Apollo broke through Clint's sphincter, Clint gave a deep sigh and said, "Oh yes that feels good. That's what I've wanted."

Apollo started moving the sling so that it swung towards him, allowing his cock to go deeply into Clint, and then away so that his cock almost popped out of Clint's ass. This backward and forward movement went on for some time with both Apollo and Clint groaning in ecstasy. All this time, I had been watching through the window, rubbing my erection in my shorts.

Something made Clint look up towards the window and he saw me.

"What the fuck are you doing here?" he shouted.

Immediately Apollo stopped his thrusts to look and see who Clint was shouting at. When he saw me at the window, he laughed and said, "What are you doing out there, why don't you come in and join us?"

Apollo pulled his cock out of Clint, untied Clint's legs and arms, and came and opened the front door. He didn't care that anyone might see his roaring hard-on, but stood in the doorway, stark naked with an erection and welcomed me in. I followed him into the room and found Clint sitting on the wooden bed.

"How did you get here?" asked Clint.

"I got a lift in a fishing boat," I replied. "And, what are you doing here? Couldn't get enough?"

"You've got room to talk," he said.

Apollo intervened and told us to shut up and stop arguing. He then moved over to the wooden bed and sat down on the edge.

"Come, Clint, sit on me," he said, and holding his firm cock in his right hand, he spread his legs for Clint to move in between them. Clint moved over to Apollo almost as if being magnetically drawn to him and positioned himself with his back to Apollo and slowly lowered his ass-hole onto Apollo's dick. I watched as the whole of Apollo's cock disappeared into Clint's ass. Clint rested his back against Apollo's chest and began to rise and fall on Apollo's cock. At first Clint did this slowly, savoring every movement, but then sometimes he would raise himself from Apollo's cock so that just the tip of Apollo's cock was inside him, and then let himself fall onto the erect cock. Every time he did this there was a slapping sound as his ass hit Apollo's balls, and every time Clint let out a loud grunting sound. As Clint lay back against Apollo's chest and let Apollo's cock go its full length into him, Apollo thrust his hips up, fucking into Clint's ass. I could see how much Clint was enjoying this.

I moved closer and knelt in front of Clint. I put my index finger into my mouth and wet it with saliva; then I took it out and placed my finger at the entry to Clint's ass, where Apollo's cock was. I slowly started to insert my finger along the ridge of Apollo's cock. Apollo could feel my finger sliding over his cock and Clint could feel that there was something extra entering him and stretching his ass a little wider. All the time, Apollo kept up his movement and both their groans became louder. I gently inserted a second finger and joined in with Apollo's movement, in and out of Clint's ass. By this time, Clint was now writhing on Apollo's cock, meeting every thrust that Apollo made.

"Fuck me! Fuck me deeper!" cried Clint. "I want your balls up there. I want you inside me! Fuck me harder!"

Apollo obliged willingly.

Clint was enjoying this feeling. I leant over and dribbled some of my saliva onto Clint's cock. Then I lowered my tongue onto it and began to lick my saliva from his cock. He thrust his cock forward; "Suck it, Joe. Take it deep in your throat and suck my fucking cock dry."

I opened my mouth wide and engulfed his cock-head, then slowly sank my mouth down the shaft until I could feel his balls touch my chin. I carried on sucking Clint for some time, and then I lifted my head and looked at him. Sweat was pouring from both Clint and Apollo, who, from their expressions, were both enjoying this action immensely.

I stood up and moved to above Clint's cock. I faced Clint and he saw what I was planning and held his cock erect to allow me to slide onto him. As I did so, he gave a very loud groan and thrust his cock deep into me. Every time Apollo thrust into Clint and forced Clint's body to rise, I would push down on Clint's cock. I leant towards Clint's face and placed my mouth over his. Our tongues fought one another as we searched in each other's mouths. Saliva was dribbling from our mouths as we slobbered over each other. Clint pulled his mouth from mine and threw his head back in an effort to find Apollo's mouth.

Apollo's tongue shot out and their mouths became attached to one another's. I kissed Clint's face and stretched forward so that I could try and get my tongue into both their mouths. We were gripping onto each other with our arms as the pace of our fucking increased. I pulled my mouth from theirs and shouted, "I'm going to come; I'm going to come."

Clint, on hearing me say this, increased his thrusts, causing me to gasp and cry out as I shot my warm white cum over his stomach. I kept bouncing up and down on his cock, tightening my ass muscles as I shot my load, trying to get him to shoot.

Clint gave out a guttural cry, "I'm going to shoot!"

"Fuck me! Fuck me hard!" I shouted to him.

"Oh yes; Oh yes. Fuuck!" shouted Clint as he emptied his ample supply into me.

Apollo rammed a deep push into Clint's ass, held it for a moment and growled,

"Aaargh!" Apollo groaned and began to shoot one load after another up Clint's ass.

"Push it in deeper! Fuck me! Fuck me faster! I want everything you've got. Give it to me!" shouted Clint, grinding his ass deeper onto Apollo's cock.

Apollo pounded away at Clint's ass.

When Apollo had emptied himself in Clint, I slowly pulled myself from Clint's cock, which still remained erect for quite some time. Clint lay in Apollo's arms, breathing heavily with Apollo's cock still deeply imbedded in his ass. I leant forward and kissed both of them on their mouths.

"Are you OK?" asked Apollo.

"I feel wonderful," replied Clint. "Do you know something?" he continued, "you have the honor of being the first guy ever to fuck me."

Apollo laughed, "You're joking, aren't you?"

"No, he's not," I said. "This has been an honor for me too, to witness his first fuck." A thought suddenly crossed my mind; "that means that we can all get to your ass now, can't we?"

"Don't even think about it; this ass is reserved for special occasions with special people," said Clint winking at me, "and it's not going to happen that often, either."

Clint sat up and so did Apollo, but Clint didn't disengage himself from Apollo, rather, he swiveled himself on Apollo's cock so that he was now facing Apollo. Their mouths met in a long, lingering kiss, while Clint continued to rise and fall onto Apollo's still hard cock. As their lips parted, Apollo gave a little sigh and said, "Sorry! I tried not to let it slip out."

Clint rose from sitting on Apollo and I could see Apollo's limp cock lying across his left leg. Clint and I held out our hands to help him up and the three of us went off to take a shower.

"Tell me something," said Clint, looking deeply at Apollo, "was it you at the party the other night with Konstantin?"

Apollo smiled.

"Why do you ask?" he answered.

"Because I thought it might be you," I said. "Was I right?"

Apollo smiled once more.

"You're a sharp one, aren't you, Joe. Yes it was me."

"I thought so."

"And you and Brad were watching me, weren't you?" continued Apollo.

When he said that, I became embarrassed, knowing that we'd been caught out.

"Hey it's OK. I like an audience when I'm having sex," said Apollo, realizing my embarrassment.

"So why didn't you say something to us?" enquired Clint.

"I had promised Konstantin to be his master for the night and although I would have loved having a scene with you guys that night, I kept my promise."

"So it was Konstantin's lucky night?" remarked Clint.

"Yes, but today was your lucky day," responded Apollo.

"Not lucky," answered Clint. "I was determined to come back for you. There was something that was attracting me to you and I wanted to be fucked, but by you and not just anyone. Sorry, it's just something that I can't explain."

"You mean like being my slave?" commented Apollo.

"I suppose you might say that," replied Clint.

We spent the rest of the time with Apollo until my fishing boat came to pick us up. Clint and I bade him farewell and set sail for Mykonos. As we sailed back towards the island, neither Clint nor I said anything; we just had contented looks on our faces and every now and then, I caught a smile appearing on Clint's face.

When we arrived back at Vasilis' house, both he and Brad were there. "Where have you two been?" they echoed.

"Out and about," I said nonchalantly.

"I don't believe you," said Brad, "you've probably been up to mischief again!"

"Would we ever?" said Clint with a twinkle in his eyes.

"When you two get together, anything is possible," said Brad.

"I suppose that is true," laughed Clint. "Let's just say, we've been paying homage to the Greek God, Apollo."

"You bastards," shouted Brad, "and you didn't take us."

"I'll tell you about it later, much later," said Clint putting an arm around Brad, "after all, you are my best friend and I think that you have a right to know."

He winked at me and I just smiled. I wasn't quite sure how Brad was going to take this "earth shattering" news.

CHAPTER 11

CRUISING

Vasilis had spoken to Konstantin, who had a friend with a yacht, and had arranged for us to go out on the yacht one day.

"I have a surprise for you guys," said Vasilis one morning. "Get dressed and get your bathing costumes because we're going out for the day."

"Why, what have you arranged?" asked Brad, a little skeptically.

"Don't you worry about a thing," answered Vasilis. "All you need are your beach towels, costumes and suntan lotion – plenty of it."

"Oh, I know," I chirped. "We're off to another beach."

"No, you're wrong," replied Vasilis.

"So where are we going?" enquired Clint, "back to Delos and Apollo?"

The mention of the name 'Apollo' sent a tingle of excitement from my brain to my crotch and I could feel the start of an arousal.

"No," answered Vasilis, once more. "You are going sailing."

"Sailing!!" came a chorus from the three of us.

"Yes. I have arranged with a friend of Konstantin's and he's taking us out in his yacht for the day."

This was different and besides, we couldn't afford to hire a yacht, so if someone was willing to take us out, that was even better.

"Where are we going?" asked Brad.

"Wherever we want to go," said Vasilis, still smiling from ear to ear with excitement.

"I saw this beautiful cove near Super Paradise," I said, remembering the day I wandered up to the top of the cliff at the beach. "Do you think we could go there?"

"I'm sure he'll take us there. In fact, we can go right around the island, if you wish."

Suddenly we became like small children about to go out to a funfair or such like. We grabbed our towels, costumes and were about to look for some fruit or food, when Vasilis stopped us and told us that all the drinks and food would be supplied on the yacht. This was a bonus for us and made the whole idea even more exciting. While we were busy getting our things, Vasilis's mother came in to tell us that our transport to the harbor had arrived. A truck, looking a little worse for wear waited for us outside of their home and behind the wheel was a rugged looking man of about forty. We ran out to the truck and were about to clamber into the back when Vasilis stopped us.

"First let me introduce you guys to George our host."

George was the driver and obviously the owner of the yacht. We politely greeted George and thanked him in advance for offering to take us on his yacht, and then we clambered into the back while Vasilis climbed into the cab with George, and off we went.

Sitting in the back of an open truck traveling over Mykonos's dusty roads was not fun. The dust was swirling around us and by the time we reached the harbor; we had all become a little more 'tanned' from the dust.

"I think we're going to need a swim to clean ourselves up," suggested Clint, looking rather grubby.

Vasilis and George laughed heartily when they saw our dusty, dirty faces.

"Don't worry, once we get on board, you can clean up," said George, having parked his truck and leading us to the quay where his yacht was moored.

The yacht itself was a fair size with ample deck space to lie and tan on, and there was an equally ample space below deck with toilet a smallish cabin if one needed to have a sleep, a small kitchen area and a dining area. We all put our bags in the sleeping cabin and slipped into our bathing costumes and headed back on deck. George was busy easing the yacht from its moorings and soon we were headed out of the harbor and heading towards Super Paradise beach. The sea was flat and the yacht seemed to glide through the water without any rocking or rolling. We found ourselves space on the deck, threw down our towels and began to enjoy the gentle breeze and the warm sun.

"This is awesome," said Brad. "Did you tell George about the cove you wanted to go to?"

"No, but I think that Vasilis told him. Well, at least I hope so."

Vasilis had positioned himself in the front of the yacht and was lying facing the blue sky, tanning, when Brad went and put his towel down next to him.

"Can I lay here next to you, Vasilis?" enquired Brad.

"Of course you can," replied Vasilis, opening his eyes.

Clint, in the meantime, came and lay down next to me.

"This is what I call heaven," said Clint lying down on his back and resting on his elbows as he watched the island pass by.

"You're right there," I answered. "I've often dreamed of sailing the Greek islands but never thought I'd get to do it – you know, not having the money to hire a yacht."

"I think it's pretty good of Vasilis to organize this for us," remarked Clint.

We lay there not saying much more to each other, until Clint lay down on his back and, looking up at the all-encompassing blue sky, said, "Joe, do you think of Apollo at all?"

I was somewhat surprised by Clint's comment, but it did make me think.

"It's funny that you should ask me that, because I do. What about you?"

"Often, but I've never thought of someone like that before."

"Me neither," I replied. "It was funny when we were at the masked party and Brad and I wandered off and saw Konstantin with Apollo …"

"… funny in what way?"

"When I watched him fucking Konstantin, I felt magnetically drawn to him. I wanted to be the person being fucked but I haven't felt that feeling with others when I've been voyeuristic."

"You mean when you're watching two guys making out it doesn't turn you on?" asked Clint.

"Oh yes, it does, but I don't necessary want to join in or imagine I was the other party. No watching him was different, but I can't exactly explain how."

"I think I know how you feel. I can't explain why I was so drawn to go back to Delos that day but I know I just wanted him to screw me, and I've never felt that for anyone."

"I know, that ass of yours is off limits to all," I jokingly replied.

"How do you think Brad feels?" asked Clint.

"What, about you?"

"No, about Apollo. Do you think he might feel the same way that we do?"

"I don't know; he's never said anything to me, but you never know. Maybe that night with Apollo, although he was drugged, he might have been enjoying the feeling."

"Maybe," said Clint, almost contemplatively, "but I don't think so. To me he seemed to be more in pain than enjoyment. It's just that I can't place my finger on the problem. Hey, when I say problem, I don't mean it like that. What I wish I knew was why I was so drawn to him."

Maybe it's just his physique that we're attracted to," I suggested.

Clint thought for a while, and then said, "I don't think so. It's more than that. I've seen guys back in the gym who are better built than Apollo, but I'm not attracted to them in the way I am with him."

"The way I feel is that I would do anything he asked me to do," I added. "If he asked me to jump off this yacht now, I'd probably do it."

"And if he asked you to spread your legs for him...?"

"I'd do it," I laughed.

"So would I," said Clint, almost silently.

"What are you two so engrossed in?" shouted Brad, walking towards Clint and me.

"We're just saying how wonderful it was of Vasilis to organize this trip for us," said Clint, casually.

"You're right there, but he said I must tell you that we're nearing the cove you wanted to visit, Joe."

Both Clint and I sat up to see exactly where we were, and there was the cove I had admired, getting closer.

"Wow! That's an awesome beach," said Clint, standing up to get a better view. "And not a soul on it."

George took the yacht as close to the beach as he could and then dropped anchor.

"If you guys want to swim to shore you can as it's not too far," said George, pulling off his shirt to reveal a mat of dark hair on his burly chest. "I'm going for a swim," he said, pulling off his shorts to reveal a black Speedo and dived into the cool, turquoise water.

"Come on in," he shouted as he surfaced.

We never needed another invitation and soon we were all in the beautifully cooling water. We all swam to the deserted beach with its soft, white sand and lay down to dry. Silence reigned and it felt so peaceful to have no other tourists or locals around. We'd left our towels on the yacht so our wet bodies lay casually on the warm, dry sand – Brad, Clint and me together, while Vasilis lay alongside George. No one spoke and the only sound was the gentle lapping of small waves on the water's edge.

After some time, I broke the silence but not loud enough for George and Vasilis to hear.

"Brad, can I ask you something?"

"Sure. What is it?"

"What do you feel about Apollo?"

"Meaning?"

"Well, do you have any feeling towards him?"

Brad remained silent for quite a long time, and then he spoke up.

"I don't know, and I'm not trying to avoid your question, but I can't explain."

Clint and I cast a glance towards each other.

"You can't explain what?" I asked.

"I don't know how to explain it, but yes I do have some sort of feeling – like I would do anything for him."

Again Clint and I looked at each other, and then silence reigned once more.

"Why do you ask?" enquired Brad.

"No special reason. I was just wondering."

"Were you wondering if I was going to have some sort of fling with him?"

"No, nothing like that."

"So why did you ask?"

"Because we feel the same way as you do," interjected Clint, who had remained silent, listening to our conversation.

"Oh!" was all Brad could say.

"I think you've summed it up, Brad, when you said you'd do anything for him. Why?"

"Why what?"

"Why would you do anything for him?" I asked.

"I can't explain," said Brad after some thought.

Silence loomed once more.

"I'm going for a swim," said Clint rising, and running to the water's edge, sand falling from his back as he ran.

Soon we were all back in the water trying to cool down, until George suggested we get back to the yacht and head off to another beach or cove. We clambered aboard and set sail, without another word of Apollo being mentioned.

Although no words were said about Apollo, I began to wonder if he had some sort of spell on us and why we were all so eager to please him. Or, was it that we wanted to be pleased by him? Was it something in our characters that we found lacking and thought that Apollo had that missing element that we so desired? I couldn't speak for the others, but I knew that I could happily be his slave if we had been living in the fifth century when slaves existed in Greece. I was also sure that both Clint and Brad would have sold themselves to be at Apollo's beck and call, if the truth be known.

As our yacht sailed between the islands of Delos and Mykonos, I think the three of us all looked towards Delos in the hopes of seeing Apollo, but none spoke.

Our day was so relaxing and, after a hearty lunch of Greek salads and light snacks, we all relaxed like contented animals, on the deck. Vasilis went down below deck and had a sleep in the cabin and I did notice that at one stage George disappeared below deck and was gone for quite some time before reappearing together with Vasilis. Whatever happened down there, I was sure that Vasilis had enjoyed himself.

As the yacht neared the harbor on our return, four tired young men had enjoyed a peaceful and relaxing day on the still seas around Mykonos and we were grateful to both Vasilis and George for taking the time to spoil us. We thanked George and he drove us back to Vasilis's home where we once again had to shower to get rid of all the dust from being in the back of the truck – but we were all happy.

CHAPTER 12

VASILIS' FAREWELL

On our last evening on Mykonos, the four of us went out for a farewell dinner at one of the waterfront tavernas, and after spending quite a few hours chatting, eating and drinking, we headed for a last night out at one of the clubs. The four of us danced with each other and had a wonderful evening. At one stage when Clint and Vasilis were on the dance floor together, I said to Brad, "Did Clint tell you what happened to him on Delos?"

"Yes," he replied, "but somehow I can't believe it."

'Trust me, it's true; I was there to see it and be part of it."

"You mean he actually allowed Apollo to fuck him; to push his big dick into Clint?"

"Absolutely, and the funny thing was that Clint actually enjoyed it," I replied.

"Do you think this trip has converted him?" asked Brad.

I laughed, "Never in a thousand years; Clint's a top guy, unless of course he's in the mood to take on Apollo!"

"I'm going to miss you guys when you go," said Vasilis, as the night sped on.

"We're also going to miss you and the fun we've had with you," I answered.

"But most of all, I'm going to miss you, Vasilis," said Brad, "not only for your friendship, but also for bringing the guys to find me on Delos. If you hadn't been around, I might still be living on Delos with Apollo as his slave."

Vasilis smiled and added, "with all due respect, I don't think any of us would have minded being his slave, so long as he didn't have to drug you."

"Well, the only one who's going to benefit will be Vasilis," commented Clint. "At least whenever you feel like a little discipline, you can catch a boat to Delos and spend a night or two there."

"Actually that sounds like a good idea," laughed Vasilis, as he thought about his potential prospects.

As the evening came to a close, the four of us made our way back to Vasilis' house and began packing our bags for the return journey and then collapsed onto our bed. Brad, Clint and I lay on top of our bed, because it was too hot to get under the sheets, and Vasilis went off to his room. We lay there for some time chatting to each other and saying how much we had enjoyed the evening and what fun it had been having Vasilis as our host, after all, we could have booked into a hotel and none of our adventures might have happened.

While we were lying in the darkened room chatting, Clint suddenly said, "Brad, I hope you're not upset that I let Apollo screw me!"

"Why should I be upset?" came the reply. "It just means that there's hope for Joe or I to get to screw you as well then, now that you're available!"

I burst out laughing; "I never thought of it like that," I said, "but you've got a point there, Brad. Should we do it to him now? You first, then I'll slip into him!"

"Don't even think about it," came a deep growl from Clint.

The three of us cuddled up next to each other and eventually fell asleep.

When we woke in the morning and opened our eyes, we found that during the night Vasilis had come into the room, crept onto the bed and snuggled up next to us, so that the four of us woke to find our arms tangled around one another. We lay there for some time hugging and kissing each other, feeling our cocks getting harder.

Vasilis broke away from us, leapt from the bed and said, "I want to give you all something to remember me by."

We all looked bewildered as we had no idea what Vasilis had in mind.

"Brad, I want you to lie in the opposite direction from Clint so that your feet are where his head is and vice versa," resumed Vasilis, as though directing traffic. "You will have to cover his legs with yours, Brad. Now Joe, I want you to lie next to them. You can lie in the same direction as Clint or Brad; it doesn't matter."

I did as I was told and suddenly realized what Vasilis had planned. With Brad and Clint laying the way they were, Clint's massive cock came up between Brad's legs so that both their cocks were next to each other; and with me lying next to Clint, I was able to get my cock close to the other two.

"Now I will take you," said Vasilis running his wet tongue over all three cocks. He licked the heads of our cocks, and opening his mouth as wide as he could, began to take Brad's and Clint's cocks into his mouth. He forced both cock-heads into his mouth and ran his tongue over them. I don't know whether anyone had done this to Brad or Clint before, but watching this being done, turned me on, just as much as it turned them on. They were both thrusting their cocks up into Vasilis' mouth, trying to force their way down his throat. After trying to sink down their cock shafts, Vasilis raised his head and moved over to take my cock into his mouth. While he sucked on me, Clint took hold of both his and Brad's cock's with his mighty hands and began to shunt his hands up and down their cocks. They were wet from Vasilis' saliva, so there was little friction; his hands just moved smoothly and slickly over their huge dicks.

Vasilis went back to their cocks and once again, opened his mouth, but this time I noticed he was able to take in more of them. He was able to slide his mouth probably a quarter of the way down their cocks. Both Brad and Clint began to thrust their cocks into Vasilis' mouth, fucking his face. As I watched them I stroked my own hard-on, sliding my hand up and down my saliva-greased cock. Watching them was making me very horny and I could feel myself getting closer to shooting.

My breathing became heavier and I started working my cock faster. I saw Vasilis look at me from the corner of his eye as he sucked the other two. Realizing that I was getting close, he removed his mouth from their cocks and slammed it onto mine. My cock sank deep into his throat.

"Aaargh!" I groaned as he did that. "Suck it! Suck my dick." I started fucking his face. "Take this big dick! Oh Fuck! Suck me dry! Fuck, what a cocksucker! I'm goin' to shoot my load! Oh yes! Oh Fuck! It's coming! Aargh! Suck me! Fuck me! Oh yes!"

As I shot a heavy load into Vasilis' mouth, I could feel him swallowing my hot cum. He kept up his movement, going up and down my cock and I could feel another load shoot down his throat. He wrapped his lips tightly around my cock and sucked, draining every last drop of cum from my dick. Then, when he knew that there was nothing left in my dick, he slowly slid his mouth up the shaft, reached the tip of my cock and ran his tongue over the tip.

I shivered, "Oh Fuck that's good!" I said.

He kissed the tip of my cock and moved over to Brad and Clint who had been watching his action with much interest and had been stroking their own cocks the whole time. Vasilis sank his mouth over their cocks and proceeded to slide his mouth up and down them. While he did this, I slipped under Vasilis and took his erect cock into my mouth and started to give him a blowjob. Vasilis was grunting muffled sounds as he sucked Brad and Clint, and saliva was dribbling from the corners of his mouth as he saturated their dicks, making it easier for him to slide deeper onto them.

Every time his mouth went down their shafts, they pushed upwards groaning in ecstatic unison. Brad could feel his cock rubbing against Clint's every time Vasilis' mouth closed on them. Brad was the first to give an indication that he wasn't going to be able to hold on much longer.

"I'm getting close; I don't think I can hold on much longer," he said.

"So am I," said Clint. "Oooh! Fuck, I'm coming! I'm goin' to shoot."

"Oh God, I'm coming!" exclaimed Brad.

His body tensed and he gave a grunt. "Aaaargh!" and they both began to shoot into Vasilis' mouth.

Vasilis tried as best he could to stay plugged onto their cocks because they were both fucking his mouth at the same time.

"Fuckin' hell! Take my dick! Suck it hard! Harder!" shouted Clint.

"Deeper!" yelled Brad. "Suck my fat cock. Oh yes!"

Both of them were fighting for space in Vasilis' mouth. They were both trying to force their entire shaft down his throat, and Vasilis was trying his best to take their whole shafts. Cum was spilling from Vasilis' mouth as he was battling to swallow it all.

As the two guys continued to pump his throat, I tightened my grip on Vasilis' cock and increased my sucking. He gave a muffled groan and I felt the first shots of his hot cum shoot into my mouth. I swallowed and gobbled on his cock, sucking as hard as I could, forcing the length of his shaft down my throat. I felt another shot of cum hit the back of my throat, and then another.

Vasilis finally let go of Brad and Clint's cocks and gave out a deep sigh; "Oh that tasted so good. I could suck you guys all day. Those are the best cocks I've ever had," he said.

Clint lay on his back, his cock still half erect and said, "Better than Apollo's?"

"When I'm with Apollo, there's only one, but when I'm with you guys, there are three cocks."

"Have you done this before?" asked Brad.

"No, why do you ask?" came the reply.

"Well the fact that you could take a nine-inch as well as a ten-inch cock in your mouth at the same time. That must take some practice!"

"I promise this is the first time I have tried that. It's just that I couldn't resist trying to have you both at the same time. I hope you liked what you got, because I would hate you to leave Greece with unhappy memories."

"If anything," I said, "I think we'll be back for more next year."

"That's for sure," said Clint. "So between now and then, Vasilis, we want you to practice more, so that next time you will be able to take all three cocks at the same time."

The man would be a genius if he could do that, I thought.

We showered and finally had breakfast, then we got our things together, said goodbye to Vasilis' mother and thanked her, and Vasilis took us down to the harbor to catch the ferry back to Piraeus.

We hugged and kissed each other and then boarded our ferry. With a loud 'toot' on the ship's horn we were about to depart. We waved goodbye to Vasilis as the ship set sail, and once he was out of sight, we then went and found ourselves some deck chairs to relax in.

The three of us were exhausted, so throughout the journey we kept dozing off to sleep and then being woken up by the noise of the passengers. We all had Speedos under our shorts, so after we had been woken up a few times, we pulled our shorts off and lay in the blazing sun tanning our bodies.

While we lay there, I noticed how many young men walked past and took long admiring looks at us. At one point, I looked over towards Clint, who was lying on the other side of Brad, and noticed that he was asleep again, but had the most enormous hard-on in his Speedo – no wonder the young men were admiring him! Every now and then, his hand would run across the huge bulge in his costume, stroking his cock, and Brad and I would look at each other and snigger, but at no stage were we going to stop him, after all, he was obviously having beautiful thoughts.

As we neared Piraeus, the ferry began to slow down and Brad tapped Clint on his hard cock, and said, "I think it's time for you to wake up and for that to go to sleep."

Clint opened his eyes, looked around him and then looked down at his erection, stretched his legs out in front of himself and rubbed his hands over his cock. A couple of young men who had been admiring him throughout the journey, smiled when they saw how hard his erection was.

"Hmmmm! That was good," sighed Clint, and smiled.

"Who were you thinking of?" I asked.

He smiled, turning to us, "You'll never know!"

CHAPTER 13

ATHENS BY NIGHT

The ferry docked and we collected our things together, pulled on our shorts and disembarked.

"Hello," shouted a familiar voice, above the surrounding sounds.

"That has to be Dimitri," said Brad, without actually seeing him.

The little man rushed up to greet us as we had walked the gangway.

"Welcome back," he said, shaking our hands and hugging us as though we had been away for years. "I am ready to take you to your hotel," he said picking up as much luggage as he could manage and putting it into his beaten up old car.

We had booked into the same hotel that we had stayed at on our arrival, and so, once again we played with our lives as his car sped through the streets leading to the center of Athens. Throughout the journey to the hotel, Dimitri wanted to know in detail what we had done on Mykonos during our stay there. Naturally, without discussing it amongst ourselves, we left out certain details, which we thought wouldn't be of importance to him.

"You meet many nice people there?" asked Dimitri, enthusiastically.

"Oh yes," I replied.

"You have naughty time there?" enquired our self-appointed driver with a glint of mischief in his eyes.

We looked to each other and then Brad answered for us.

"Oh yes, you can't go to Mykonos without having a naughty time."

Dimitri seemed pleased with Brad's answer and then added, "But you had a good time?"

"Oh yes," we all echoed, and then Brad and I muttered under our breath, "especially Clint."

Clint smiled at us knowingly and said, "I'd be careful what I say, or I could embarrass you two."

"Come off it, Clint, nothing embarrasses us," said Brad.

We continued this banter until we finally reached the hotel, unloaded the car and booked in to the hotel. What a pleasure to be back out of the intense heat and in the coolness of the hotel room.

Since our stay on Mykonos, we had made enquiries and found out about a couple of bars, clubs and saunas in Athens, and as we were only spending two nights in Athens before our flight home, we decided to "hit the town" that night.

Dimitri asked if we wanted him to drive us anywhere, but we declined, saying that we wanted to walk about the streets.

We spent the rest of the day wandering around the streets of Athens looking at the various shop windows, buying a few typical tourist souvenirs and surveying the array of young Greek men who were also wandering the streets. We made our way towards Syntagma Square to watch the guard where, naturally, Brad and I embarrassed Clint by trying to look under the soldiers "frilly skirts" as they lifted their legs high into the air as they marched, but we couldn't see what they were wearing underneath.

Eventually, Clint said, "I reckon one of you had better pick up a soldier, then you can ask him what they wear under those things;

or better still, why don't you go up to one of these soldiers and ask him to bend over so that you can see for yourself."

"That's not a bad idea," I said, and pretended to go towards the soldiers on parade.

"I'm not being serious," shouted Clint.

I turned, and laughing said, "Don't worry, neither am I."

The intense heat coming up from the streets was making us hot and tired again, so we decided to wend our way back to the hotel to take a shower, cool down and rest before going out that evening.

That evening we had a light supper in the hotel and Brad said, "Well, what's the plan for tonight?

"I don't know how you guys feel," said Clint, "but I feel like going to a sauna and then having a few drinks."

"A sauna in this heat!" I exclaimed. "Are you mad?"

"Hey!" exclaimed Brad. "That sounds like a good idea. Do you mind if I go along with you?"

"Of course not. I actually didn't want to go on my own," said Clint. "What about you Joe, don't you want to come along as well?"

The fact that I didn't want to stay in the hotel alone, made me choose to join the other two. So that was agreed upon.

At about seven that evening, Dimitri arrived at the hotel, offering to take us wherever we wanted to go. We told him of our plans and he seemed quite happy to drive us to the various venues. In fact, we were a little surprised at his keenness.

First stop was a sauna called 'Athens Relax' at which, we had been told, and one could get a massage, amongst other things. Dimitri parked his car just off Omonia Square, and we made our way to the sauna.

We paid and were told where our lockers were. We found our way around and got undressed, wrapping the small white towel that was given to each of us, around our waists, then we went to explore.

There were quite a number of young men there, as well as a few older ones, but very few resembled tourists. The three of us tended to stay together as we wandered around, finding out where everything was.

We eventually found the steam room, the sauna and the swimming pool. We saw a sign, which indicated the rooms where the massages took place, and then we saw a darkened area.

Clint spoke up and said, "I believe this place has got a dark room."

"Where? Do you think this darkened area might be it?" said Brad.

"I don't know, but I'm sure that you'll find it," replied Clint.

Eventually, having found most of the facilities, we started going our separate ways. I went into the steam room, which seemed to be packed with bodies moving slowly through the steam. Once my eyes became accustomed to the limited light in there, I could see people walking by and touching each other. I could also hear slurping sounds as people were sucking off others, and in one corner of the room, a couple were wrapped in each other's arms, kissing. Some still had their miniscule towels on, while others were naked. I wandered around, much like the others did and a couple of hands fondled my ass and tried to grope my crotch, but no-one took my immediate interest. After some time, when the steam became too hot, I left and went into the cool swimming pool. After having cooled my body down, I wrapped my towel around my waist again and wandered off towards the darkened area.

I eventually found the dark room that Clint had spoken of. It really was dark. I slowly entered and began to feel my way around. All one could hear was breathing, and occasionally one would touch a body and a hand might slide down to try and touch your cock. I kept moving, but wasn't sure whether I was going around in circles or not. My body bumped into another body and I put my hand out to feel in the dark. I felt a chest, which seemed well developed. I ran my hands upwards towards where the face would be and felt a smoothly shaved face. I held onto the face and directed my mouth towards his mouth. When our mouths connected, our tongues started to search in each other's mouth. I then felt that I had a connection, so I could let go of his face and use my hands to find other parts of his body. My hands slid down his wet body and came to rest on a beautifully round and firm ass. I squeezed his ass and felt him thrust his swollen cock against mine. I held him in that position for some time, then moved my hands from the back to the front and slid them in between us to take a firm grip on his cock. As I wrapped my hands around his cock, I realized that I had a very large one in my hands.

As a result of the steam, the sweat and water, my hands slid effortlessly up and down his huge erect dick. This felt good and so I slowly lowered my body, still holding onto his dick, until I was kneeling on the wet floor in front of him. I put out my tongue and ran it up the full length of his cock. He uttered a gentle moan. My mouth traveled all the way down his hard cock until I reached his balls, which I lapped with my tongue. Again, my mouth rose up his shaft until I reached the top of his cock. I ran my tongue over the tip of his cock a few times letting the tip of my tongue insert into his piss slit, then I opened my mouth wide and swallowed his entire cock all the way down to his pubic hairs, which were damp from his sweat.

This continued for some time with him fucking my face. I could feel other bodies around us; moving or touching us, but neither of us wanted to leave the other, so we remained attached to each other. I could feel hands coming in between us to try and stroke his cock, but every time a hand came near, I sank my mouth deeper around his cock. Neither of us spoke, but from our actions, we knew what the other wanted. I kept up the pace until I felt his balls moving as though they were rising up his stomach, getting ready to shoot their load. He held my head still and proceeded to pound my mouth until I heard a groan come from him and felt the first splatter of his cum hit the back of my throat. He just kept pounding away at my mouth, offloading as much as he had in him. When I felt him begin to relax, his hands left my head, but my mouth stayed glued to his cock as I slowly drew my mouth up his shaft, draining whatever remained, out of him. Throughout this process he had groaned and moaned in pleasure. I thought that he would simply leave, having been satisfied, but he didn't. Instead, he lifted me to my feet and I felt him go down on his knees and wrap his mouth around my throbbing cock. He sucked beautifully. It was done with passion and feeling. With his mouth tightly clamped around my cock, it didn't take long for me to reach a climax as I had worked myself up while I sucked him off.

"I'm going to come! Oh suck me dry!" I whispered.

I could hear others in the room also getting worked up and the noise level had risen, like so many other things, quite rapidly since the two of us had got together. I let fly my load with a low groan of pleasure, and he drank every drop down his throat as he milked me dry. Eventually, when I had nothing left inside of me, I reciprocated by gently lifted him from the floor onto his feet, felt for his face again, and kissed him. I could taste my cum in his mouth, and no doubt, he could taste his in my mouth, but our kisses were passionate. When our mouths parted, he held me in his arms, hugging me and then he said, "Thanks Joe that was terrific."

"Clint!" I exclaimed, "Is that you?"

"Who else has a cock like this?"

"But how did you know it was me?" I asked.

"I would know that kiss and that cock anywhere," replied Clint.

We both burst out laughing, and holding hands, left the dark room. We made our way to the showers and cleaned ourselves, still laughing as we did so. On the way there, we bumped into Brad.

"What are you two laughing about?" he enquired.

"Have you been to the dark room, yet?" I asked

"No," came the reply. 'Why do you ask?"

"Well we've just come from there, and it's actually quite an entertaining place," I said, and both Clint and I burst out laughing again.

"You see," said Clint, "it's so dark, you can't see anything, and it just so happened that even though there were a number of guys in there, Joe and I happened to feel each other up and have some sex, without us initially realizing who the other person was."

"You mean, of all the people in that room, you had to pick each other?" asked Brad.

"Yep," I replied. "Obviously we can sniff each other out anywhere."

"Have you scored?" Clint asked Brad.

"No, not yet, but I did see quite a nice guy heading towards the steam room; maybe I should head that way while you two get your breath back."

"Well don't be too long, because there are still other places to visit," said Clint dragging me off to find some refreshments.

Brad arrived at the steam room and opened the door. Steam gushed out to greet him as he entered and it took a little time for his eyes to adjust to the dim light. Once he had got used to the light, he looked around the room, only to find that he was there alone with the guy he had seen earlier. He sat down on one of the benches across from the guy. Neither spoke and only the hissing of the steam was evident. Trickles of sweat began to run down Brad's body and he wiped it off with his hands. The heat increased and so did his sweat. The more he rubbed from his body, the more sweat seemed to appear. His hands ran down the length of his torso and over his cock. He kept his hands on his cock for a while to see if there would be a reaction from the other guy. He noticed that the other guy did likewise. Brad then rose to his feet, rubbed his hands over his body again and flicked the sweat onto the floor. The other guy looked up at Brad as he did this. He could see Brad's dick sticking out in front of him. Brad was standing close enough for him to stretch out his hand and grab hold of Brad's cock, and pull him closer. When Brad was standing in front of the other guy, the guy opened his mouth and took Brad's cock into the warm caverns of his mouth. Brad groaned with delight and thrust his hips forward gently.

"Do you speak English?" asked Brad.

The guy kept his mouth wrapped around Brad's cock and grunted that he did.

"What's your name? Mine's Brad."

The guy released his grip, said "Marc" and promptly wrapped his mouth around Brad's cock again.

Brad thought that Marc was obviously a man of very few words.

"What do you like doing?" Brad asked, still whispering.

Again the mouth was removed.

"Sucking and fucking," came the reply, and back he went to work again.

"I like that too," said Brad, "but sometimes I also like to be fucked."

The mouth continued as though Marc hadn't heard, then the mouth slid from Brad's cock and said, "Would you like that now?"

"You mean here in the steam room?" said Brad.

"Why not! You're hot and I'm hot, so what's a little more steam?"

Marc spread his legs wide and leaned back on the bench. Brad felt Marc's cock and could feel the droplets of sweat running down it. He could also feel that he was uncut. Brad felt the trickles of sweat run down the crack of his ass, lubricating his asshole. He eased himself over Marc's erect dick and slowly lowered himself onto it. He could feel Marc's foreskin roll back and as it did so and slid into Brad, Marc gave a deep sigh of contentment. Brad was now sitting astride Marc's legs, facing him and riding up and down on Marc's sweaty dick. Their hot, sweat- covered chests rubbed against each other as Brad continued his up and down movement. Marc simply stretched out on the bench, while Brad did all of the work.

Brad wriggled his ass on Marc's dick as though he was trying to get it deeper into him, and started kissing Marc at the same time. Their tongues fought a duel in each other's mouth, and all the time Brad rode as though he were riding a horse. Suddenly the door to the steam room opened and someone walked in.

Brad froze on top of Marc's stiff cock. Should he get off and pretend nothing had been happening, or should he just carry on? Before he had a chance to make up his mind, he felt Marc thrust his cock upwards into Brad's ass, obviously suggesting that they carry on. Brad continued with his movements up and down, and as they began to become more frantic and fast, he could see that the new guy in the room was stroking his hard-on as he watched them.

Brad could feel himself nearing a climax so his riding became even more frenzied until it was as though he was riding a bucking bronco at a rodeo. Both he and Marc were sweating profusely and their groans and grunts were becoming louder and more regularly.

Brad's breathing was getting heavier as he rode Marc's throbbing cock. He pounded up and down, sweat flying from them in all directions until he shouted, "I'm goin' to come! Oh Fuck, I'm goin' to shoot."

"Shoot!" came the response. "So am I."

Both Marc and Brad started shooting their loads at the same time. Brad could feel the warm cum flying into his ass, as for the first time Marc actually started thrusting his cock deeper into Brad, lifting his ass and pelvis from the bench. As he did so, Brad met him with his own downward thrusts onto Marc's cock.

When they had emptied themselves, and their breathing had become less labored, Brad relaxed with Marc's cock still inside of him and leant forward rubbing his stomach and chest over Marc's where his cum had splayed. As he used his chest to rub the cum over both of them, the movement caused his ass muscles to clamp around Marc's cock, as though he were determined not to let it get away.

While they had been reaching their climax, the new guy in the room had moved closer to watch the action and had stroked his own dick to a climax, which he had shot over Brad's back. Brad lay in the arms of Marc while the new guy rubbed his cum over Brad's back and down towards Brad's ass where Marc's cock was still imbedded. He inserted a wet finger into Brad's ass and Brad wriggled his ass as he felt both Marc's cock and the new guy's finger inside of him. Exhausted from the exercise and the heat of the steam room, Brad slowly stood up, allowing Marc's dick to slide gently from him.

"I need a cold shower," said Brad.

"So do I," said Marc, and the two of them left the steam room and headed for the showers, leaving the stranger to his own devices.

After showering and cooling down, Brad joined Clint and I for a cold drink and proceeded to tell us all about his steam room escapade. Being content that we had all been sexually satisfied, we showered, dressed and headed out into the night to find Dimitri patiently waiting for us in his car.

"Did you all enjoy yourselves?" he asked.

The reply was unanimous, and we were sure that Dimitri knew just what went on in the sauna without us having to elaborate on the details for him.

Now we were ready to go and have a couple of drinks, relax and then head back to the hotel for a good night's rest.

Dimitri took us to a bar in the Kolonaki area, which had a disco downstairs and a cruising bar upstairs. As we had already done our cruising, we chose to go to the downstairs bar to listen to the music, do a bit of dancing and generally relax. At this bar, Dimitri chose to come with us rather than sit in the car. There were a lot of young guys in this particular bar, and Brad and I decided that we should encourage Dimitri to take a little interest in some of these young men, so we spent the night trying to play matchmaker.

"What do you think of that guy, Dimitri?" asked Brad, pointing to a young man of about early twenties sitting near us.

Dimitri surveyed the young man and said, "Too fat."

We all looked in dismay as the man didn't come anywhere near to being fat, so we tried another approach.

"If you think he's too fat, at least then when you make love, you have something to hold onto," suggested Clint.

Dimitri merely screwed up his face.

"Dimitri, if you had to choose a guy in this bar, other than us, which one would you choose?" I asked.

Dimitri's eyes wandered around the bar, and then he stopped and stared. We tried to follow his stare but were unsure which man he was looking at.

"Which one?" asked Brad?

"The one in the blue shirt and the short, dark hair," replied Dimitri.

We all looked and agreed that the guy actually was quite good looking.

"Why don't you buy him a drink?" suggested Clint.

"And then?" enquired Dimitri.

"Well maybe go up to the cruising bar and maybe he'll follow," continued Clint.

Dimitri was very hesitant, so Clint took it upon himself to order a drink for the guy and told the barman to tell the young man it was from Dimitri.

The drink was duly delivered and the young man smiled at us as the barman pointed in our direction having told him who had sent the drink. The young man raised his glass to us and then left his seat and began to walk upstairs.

"There you go, Dimitri, follow him," encouraged Clint.

As the young man started to head upstairs, he turned and smiled to us, but I thought he was smiling at Clint and not Dimitri.

Immediately, Dimitri was out of his seat and was hastily following the young man upstairs.

"I think we might have a problem," I suggested.

"Why?" asked Brad.

"I have a nagging feeling that the barman got it wrong. Because Clint paid for the drink, I think he told the young man it was from Clint and he's expecting Clint to go upstairs with him, and not Dimitri.

"Oh shit!" was all Clint could say.

There was nothing we could do, except sit and wait.

We waited and waited, but neither the young man nor Dimitri came back down.

"Do you think we should go up and see what's happening?" enquired Brad.

"Why not," said Clint and I like a chorus.

We left our drinks and headed upstairs where we found the young man on his knees giving Dimitri a blowjob. We kept our distance so as not to surprise them and watched as Dimitri stood with his trousers around his ankles, his head thrown back in ecstasy and the young man busily bringing him closer and closer to satisfaction. Once we heard Dimitri's gasps and groans, we scurried back downstairs and sat acting nonchalantly to await our driver's return.

Finally, Dimitri returned with a contented smile on his face.

"Well?" said Clint with a grin on his face. "Did you score up there?"

Dimitri grinned equally broadly and nodded his head. We all patted him on the back as though he had achieved something for the first time and offered to buy him another drink to celebrate.

The drinks flowed and Dimitri's whole attitude changed.

"Do you ever go away for a holiday, Dimitri?" asked Brad.

"Sometimes, but not always."

"And if you do where do you go?"

"To my family or my wife's family."

"Have you ever been to Mykonos?" continued Brad, "because if you want a special holiday, you should go there."

Dimitri smiled broadly.

"I think I know what you are meaning. There are nice boys there."

"Yes, and nice men," said Clint interjecting. "Go to Delos and meet Apollo; you would like him."

I tried to visualize Apollo and Dimitri together and couldn't see the connection, so I assumed that Clint was just having the poor guy on.

"Why do you say that?" enquired Dimitri.

"Because he is a man and I know you like men," said Brad.

"But I like to …you know what."

"Yes we know, you like to fuck the men," retorted Brad, "but Apollo also likes that, so maybe you two could get together."

"Stop it, Brad," I whispered, trying to get Brad to stop teasing Dimitri.

"I'm just having a bit of fun with him," replied Brad.

We finished our drinks and felt that we'd had enough to drink so we were almost ready to go back to the hotel.

By the time we decided to head for the hotel, we had noticed that Dimitri had been spending quite a lot of time still eyeing the young man he'd met upstairs.

Brad turned to Dimitri and said, "listen Dimitri, we're going back to the hotel so you can stay on if you want to."

This was not an option as far as Dimitri was concerned. "No! I'll take you back to the hotel," he said, almost like a dictator, "then I'll come back to the bar – he'll wait for me, I'm sure."

"Do you want to tell him that you're coming back, so that he waits for you?" I asked.

Dimitri didn't need to give an answer; he went straight over to the young man and said something to him that we couldn't hear or understand, and then he returned to us.

"Come, we go and then I return."

"Are you sure?" I reiterated.

We were pleased that Dimitri had found someone for himself, and although we tried to persuade him not to worry about us, he became more adamant.

Dimitri, turned to us and said, "Come, I'll take you home now," and then indicating to the young man, he said in English, "and you'll come too."

The young man seemed surprised at Dimitri's sudden change of plan, but he quickly followed.

So the three of us climbed into the back of the car while Dimitri and his young date climbed into the front. The whole way back to the hotel, Dimitri kept up an animated conversation, but at no time were we ever introduced to his date, so we never found out who he was – maybe Dimitri didn't want us to know in case one of us made a move on the young man; not that I think we would have, as we were all physically too tired to do anything, particularly have sex! However, the one nagging thought that kept flashing through my mind was what would his wife say if she knew what he was up to? However, I then thought back to what I'd learnt when I was studying and realized the Greeks had been entertaining men centuries back, so why should it change now, and although many Greek men had wives and families, it didn't stop them from having male boyfriends.

CHAPTER 14

THE LAST DAY

We got up on our last day in Greece, having thoroughly enjoyed our stay.

"Thanks, Joe, for suggesting Greece to us," said Clint, who had changed his outlook during our holiday from being a bit of a serious guy to one full of fun and willing to create fun.

"It's my pleasure, Clint, I'm glad that we were able to come here together because I don't know if I'd have as much fun if I'd been alone."

We dressed and, having packed our bags in readiness for our departure, we went downstairs for breakfast.

"So what's on the agenda today?" asked Clint.

"I don't know," I replied. "I actually hate it when it gets to the end of a holiday and we have to leave."

"Same here," echoed Brad. "I reckon I could stay here for good."

"Me too," I replied, taking a drink of water, "especially on Mykonos."

"What do you guys feel like doing today?" restated Clint.

"I don't know if I really want another day of Dimitri all day," I said, "but that's up to you. What I can suggest is that we do the short three island cruise."

"What's that?" asked Brad.

"I saw it advertised in the foyer of the hotel. It's a day trip to the islands of Hydra, Poros and Aegina by boat."

"Sounds like fun to me," said Brad, "But do you think we'll find any Apollo's on these islands?"

"Who knows, maybe we will. What do you think, Clint?"

"Sounds good to me, but how do we get there?"

"Well, let's go down to the reception desk and ask."

We finished our breakfast and went downstairs to reception where we enquired about the day trip. As luck would have it, another couple had booked the same trip so transport was already on its way to pick them up, so the receptionist phoned to find out if another three guests could be accommodated. To our relief, we could, so we paid the required fee and waited for the transport to arrive to take us back to Piraeus to catch the boat.

A small bus arrived and the five of us; a middle-aged couple and three gay men, went speeding through the bustling streets of Athens to Piraeus to board our sea transport. It was quite surprising to find that the boat we were traveling on wasn't a small means of transport that we had thought it might be, but instead a ship with at least three decks and a number of people on board. We soon established that this ship also acted as a means of transport for some of the locals traveling to and from the various islands.

As we weren't sure what to expect on our day trip, we had all put our Speedos on under our shorts and Brad carried a small backpack with our towels, bottles of water and a few pieces of fruit, in case we got hungry. As the ship left the harbor, Brad and Clint found some deck chairs and got themselves comfortable in the outdoor sunshine. I, on the other hand had decided to explore the ship and see what was on board – both activities and men!

The majority of tourists were middle-aged; however, I did find quite a few young, presentable male tourists, as well as a few eligible crew, so I reported back to Brad and Clint, who were by now dozing in the sun.

"What did you find?" asked Brad when I reached them.

"A few eligible young men, not to mention some crew members."

"Oh yes, I can see you two down in the engine room," said the dull voice of Clint, with his eyes closed.

"Actually, that's not a bad idea," remarked Brad, "so Joe, go and see if there are any decent guys who work in the engine room."

"You like a bit of grease and muck, don't you?" commented the dozy Clint again.

"Where exactly are we heading, Joe?" asked Brad.

"Apparently we head to Hydra first, then go on to Poros and finally to Aegina."

"And what's to see on each of these islands?" drawled the dozy voice of Clint.

"Talent, sea, talent, sea, talent and maybe a temple or two," I replied.

"You're having me on, aren't you, Joe?"

"Not at all. You can swim, visit the towns and shops and then on Aegina there's the Temple of Afea Athena to see, if you'd like."

"I told you before we started on this holiday I wasn't into historical things," reminded Clint.

"Well you didn't mind the ruins on Delos and the hunky archeologist that worked there did you?" I chirped in.

"That was different."

"How so? You might just find another hunky archeologist on Aegina," I suggested.

I joined Brad and Clint on the deck to bask in the sun until we docked at Hydra, which was a quaint little harbor with equally quaint narrow streets.

We disembarked and wandered around the small town area, but didn't find anything too exciting, so we headed back to the ship and went back to tanning in the sun. While we were lying there in the sun, one of the crew came up to us and asked if we were not going ashore.

"We've already been," replied Brad, "but we'd love something to drink."

"If you go down two decks, you'll find the dining room where you can buy drinks," said the crew member, whom Brad had taken a fancy to.

"I wonder if you'd mind showing me where?" asked Brad, fluttering his eyelashes at the young Greek man.

The crew member smiled and obliged. Brad leapt to his feet and was hurriedly following the young man down to the dining room.

Clint and I, in the meantime, sat on the deck waiting for Brad to bring us something to drink, other than the water we carried in our backpack. We waited and waited.

Meanwhile two decks below us, Brad and his young crew member had deviated from the dining room area and had landed up in a cabin used by the crew when they were off duty. Brad lay on the bunk while his young friend gave his swollen cock loving attention with his mouth

"Ooh, Nick," cooed Brad as the young crew member slid his mouth along the hefty length, "you suck so well."

Young Nick raised his head to smile acknowledgement to Brad and then resumed his position. Soon Brad felt he wanted to give back to the young Nick a taste of what he was receiving, so Brad swiveled around so that he could gain access to Nick's uncut cock that was throbbing in the air. Brad swallowed the young cock and sucked long and hard on it, causing the young man to sigh and moan gently.

Nick's tongue then ventured closer to Brad's asshole in search of his tight opening. The young Greek crew member found it without difficulty and inserted his tongue, causing Brad's asshole to clamp tight and quiver with excitement, but still Brad worked feverishly on Nick's throbbing cock.

"You make me come," said the young Greek, panic in his voice, but Brad was not about to stop.

Brad's mouth worked hard and tighter, making young Nick move back to Brad's cock and increase his passion on it

"I come!" cried young Nick as his Greek juices flowed into Brad's throat.

Brad never let up and swallowed as fast as Nick fired, but Brad was also getting closer to shooting.

"Oh fuck!" gasped Brad as his body tensed and his cock spewed his warm cum into Nick's mouth.

His young Greek friend wasn't expecting the flood that entered his mouth and almost gagged as it hit his throat. He immediately released his hold on Brad's cock and watched as it fired shot after shot into his face.

When both men had exhausted their supply, Brad simply cleaned the young Greek's face with his hand and then kissed Nick, which also surprised him. Maybe young Greek men were not keen on kissing thought Brad as he felt Nick withdraw. Maybe they saw having sex with another man as acceptable, but kissing was a taboo.

Once they had both cleaned up, they emerged cautiously from the cabin and went back into the dining room where Brad bought drinks for Clint and me.

"What took you so long?" asked Clint when Brad eventually surfaced back on deck.

"I was busy," replied Brad.

"Yes, we can see that. You look disheveled and that bulge in the front of your Speedo hasn't got smaller yet," said Clint, giving Brad a knowing wink.

"So who was he?" I asked.

"I don't know what he does on the ship, but I found out his name is Nick."

"Naughty, Nick the Greek," I remarked, "and what did naughty Nick do to please you?"

"Just a blowjob, that's all," said Brad casually, as though he was telling someone about things he'd bought from his shopping list.

"Just a blowjob," I repeated. "Well it couldn't have been too bad because you look very pleased with yourself."

Brad laughed loudly.

"Not as pleased as he probably is. That kid had a load on him and I took it all down without spilling a drop," said Brad proudly.

Clint never said a word, but listened intently to our conversation, giving a wry smile every now and then.

The hooter on the ship sounded and we all sat up to see the ship slowly moving away from the quay and off to Poros. We had realized that the amount of time spent in each place was minimal, so if we wanted to do or see things, we'd have to move fast.

With this in mind, we made enquiries as to what was there to do on Poros and found it was very much like Hydra, except the town was more spacious.

When we docked at Poros harbor, we decided to go on shore and see what the shops had to offer, but we soon found to our dismay that it was the same typical tourist souvenirs that you could buy anywhere in Greece. Instead of wasting our time shopping, we decided to head to the nearby beach for a swim to cool down.

The beach was very like any in the Cyclades group of islands that we had visited; barren with no shade but crystal clear cool seas. We frolicked and swan, tanned and swam again until we felt it was time to head back to the ship. At least when we arrived back at the ship, we felt a little more refreshed.

The ship headed off to our last destination, which didn't take long and while on board, we were told that this stop would be our longest.

"I made enquiries about the Temple and I think I'm going to take a look at it, if you want to join me," I said to Brad and Clint.

"We'll see when we get there," was Clint's answer, as he sprawled out on the deck in his Speedo, tanning himself.

Very soon, our ship docked and we all disembarked along with the other tourists.

"So what are you guys going to do?" I asked.

"I don't suppose there's much else to do on this island other than visit the Temple you mentioned," remarked Clint, "so I suppose we might as well tag along with you."

"I agree with Clint," added Brad. "I reckon when you've seen one island, you've seen them all."

"OK, then let's head off," I said, leading the way like a typical tour guide but without the inevitable umbrella waving in the air.

"Do you know where to go, Joe?" asked Brad, after we'd been walking for about twenty minutes.

"I hope so. This was the way I was told to go, so if we keep walking, we should get there."

"But I don't see any other tourists on the same road, Joe," observed Clint.

He was right of course; there were only the three of us, but we continued.

After about forty minutes, we arrived at a group of ruins which we thought might be the Temple. We wandered among the ruins, which were not nearly as preserved as the ones on Delos, but it still didn't deter us. As we wandered around what we thought were the ruins, Clint suddenly stopped in his tracks.

"Hey guys," he whispered, "look over there."

We looked in the direction in which he was looking and saw a well-built, shirtless man chipping away at some rocks.

"It's Apollo," said a stunned Brad.

"It can't be," I replied, "he's on Mykonos."

"It looks exactly like him; same build, same facial features, in fact everything seems the same," said Clint, still whispering.

"Let's move over there to take a closer look," suggested Brad.

The three of us moved slowly, yet without making it obvious, towards the massive man. As we neared him, Clint became more convinced that it was definitely Apollo and his face lit up with joy, but so did Brad and mine.

The man continued with his work, without looking up at us as we reached him. Clint was the first to speak.

"Apollo, is that you?" he asked.

The man raised his head and looked at us, and then he smiled.

"I am sorry, but I think you have mistaken me," replied the man.

Clint became embarrassed and couldn't stop apologizing for his error.

"We thought you were a friend we had met on Mykonos. We're so sorry," said Clint.

The giant of a man stood up and we were able to admire his muscular arms, legs and chest as he stretched his body.

"I understand now," he said, still smiling at us. "You have mistaken me for my brother, Apollo. He works on the island of Delos."

"Yes, yes, that's him," said an excited Brad.

"We are often mistaken," said the man. "My name is Zack and we are twins."

"He never said anything about having a twin," I said, "but it's nice to meet you," I continued, extending my hand to shake his.

I felt the firm grip on my hand and immediately a warm feeling emerged from my crotch. I was sure that the other two were also aroused to see a duplicate of Apollo, knowing the fun we'd had with him.

"We were looking for the Temple of Afea Athena," I said, introducing myself.

Brad and Clint also introduced themselves to Zack and we were surprised by his reaction once he knew who we were.

"This is such a small world," said Zack, laughing loudly. "Apollo telephoned me and said he had met three young Americans on holiday and that he had enjoyed such a good time with you guys, and that he was missing already."

We looked a little concerned as we had no idea how much Apollo had shared with his twin brother.

"What sort of things did Apollo tell you?" asked Clint hesitantly.

Zack grinned.

"Oh, he tells me everything, that's what twins do."

"Is that all twins do" asked Clint, returning a smile to Zack, "tell each other things?"

Zack's grin broadened

"You said you were looking for the Temple. I can show you if you wish."

This wasn't exactly the question that Clint was anticipating, but he hoped it might lead to something other than a tour of some ancient ruin.

"Yes please," I responded.

And so it was that Zack led us away from the area in which he was working and headed towards where the ruins were.

"My brother tells me you have a good ass," said Zack to Clint.

So obviously all the details were given to Zack, thought Clint.

"What else did Apollo tell you?" enquired Clint, who was walking alongside Zack, while Brad and I followed closely not wanting to miss a word of their conversation.

"He tells me you have a big cock... no he didn't say big, he said huge, massive. Is that true?"

"I don't think it's that big, but apparently some guys seem to think it is," responded Clint with modesty.

Zack smiled at Clint, winked and added, "maybe I get lucky and see?"

"Maybe," replied Clint, hoping that Brad and I wouldn't hear him.

"What about your friends here?"

Clint glanced in our direction. We had heard what Zack had said and I certainly didn't want to miss out on any potential fun and I was sure that Brad probably felt the same way, but we pretended not to have listened to their conversation.

"I'm sure they won't be a problem," said Clint, without consulting us.

Suddenly we arrived at the ruins. We had obviously been well off the track because these were worth the visit.

"I don't know if you want to wander around on your own," suggested Zack, "and then once you have spent some time here, I'll show you some other ruins we've recently uncovered."

"Sure, thanks Zack," I replied, taking Brad by the arm and leading him away from the other two.

"Why are you taking my arm like that?" questioned Brad, when we were out of earshot.

"Zack and Clint want to be alone, so I thought we could look at the ruins instead."

"What! And miss out on the fun? Are you mad!" exclaimed Brad.

"Sh! Keep your voice down. That was only a pretense. They think we've wandered off, but I've been keeping an eye on them and I saw in which direction they were headed. Come on, let's follow them," I replied.

Brad and I back-tracked to where we had left Clint and went in the direction that the two men had gone. We kept a fair distance between us and them and made sure that we were not seen, keeping quiet all the time.

"Where have they gone?" asked Brad.

I stopped and looked around. I couldn't see them, but I knew that they couldn't have just vanished.

"They must have found a room or shelter of some sorts," I concluded. "Just keep quiet in case they are nearby and they hear us."

We crept around like a pair of lions on the prowl, moving stealthily and keeping an alert look out for Clint and Zack.

"There!" said Brad in a hushed tone and pointing to our right.

I turned and looked. There was a shelter which must have been a room in the time the Temple was erected, except now it only had three walls instead of four and Zack had his arms around Clint and they were in a tight embrace, their lips locked together and their hands busily exploring each other's body. We watched as Clint's hands came to rest on Zack's firm, rounded ass and we noticed how he squeezed it and pulled Zack closer to him, obviously so that their cocks could rub together.

Brad and I huddled together in the blazing sun watching and feeling our cocks becoming aroused by the sight of Zack and Clint.

Clint's hands slid into Zack's shorts that he was wearing and suddenly Zack's mouth left Clint's and he gasped. We assumed a finger or two of Clint's had found its mark and was probing Zack.

Slowly Clint began to slide Zack's shorts down and we could see he had no underwear on. Zack's bronzed ass came into view, tight and round and then we could see Clint's fingers sink into the sweaty crack and dig into Zack's pulsating hole.

"Ah yes," moaned Zack as Clint's finger ground into the tight hole, searching for the Greek man's prostate to massage.

It didn't take Clint long to get Zack grinding his ass on Clint's fingers and groaning loudly, while Clint's mouth passionately caressed Zack's lips and their tongues fought a duel of domination.

"Fuck me," whispered Zack almost as a breath, but Clint was not ready to do that yet.

Clint removed his fingers from Zack's ass, much to the Greek's disappointment and Clint sank to his knees on the hard gravel floor, taking Zack's long, thick cock into his mouth and making love to it much like their mouths had done. Clint was determined to give Zack the treat of his life, very like he had done for Apollo.

Clint's mouth moved steadily along the hard shaft until he reached the tip where he opened his mouth wide and engulfed Zack's cock deep into his throat. Zack cried out as Clint's mouth sank down the full length and came to rest with his chin nudging Zack's hefty balls. Clint's cheeks then sank in as he sucked hard and drew his mouth along Zack's cock until he once more reached the tip.

I felt Brad grab my cock and start stroking it, but I wasn't content to have it stroked in my shorts, so I shucked them to the ground and stood naked for Brad to do with me as he pleased. I reciprocated by shoving my hand into his shorts and feeling his wet cock, which had been dribbling pre-cum and I too started stroking him.

We saw how Zack lifted Clint to his feet and then Zack proceeded to lubricate Clint's massive cock with his tongue and mouth. Once he felt he had lubricated it well and was ready to move on to the next level, Zack rose to his feet and we heard him say, "You fuck me now."

Clint smiled at his new-found Greek friend, turned him around, bent Zack over slightly, took hold of his hard cock and aimed it at Zack's waiting ass. Once Clint felt where Zack's throbbing asshole was, he let go of his cock, spread Zack's ass cheeks and pushed forward.

"Aargh!" cried Zack as Clint's thick cock began its journey into the warm Greek chute.

Zack's face was one of contorted pain and as Clint sank his cock deeper into Zack, the more furiously Brad and I stroked each other's cocks, never taking our eyes of Clint and Zack.

Once Clint had reached the depths of Zack's chute, he started his slow, rhythmic fuck which was sending Zack into another dimension. Zack's face changed rapidly from pain to delirious happiness as Clint increased his thrusts and Zack had now joined in with his own thrusts.

"Oh shit, you're getting me close, Joe," said Brad, laying a hand on mine to stop me from stroking his cock and making him come.

We watched with joy as Clint held tightly onto Zack's hips and became enthusiastic with his thrusts while Zack's long, thick cock bobbed each time Clint sank into the Greek's ass. We could see how both men seemed to be in a trance-like state and their actions seemed to have become one. Clint pulled Zack into an upright position and took his head to turn it so that Clint could access Zack's mouth and again their lips locked. For a moment they remained like this, and then we noticed that Clint released his mouth and said something to Zack.

Both men's actions increased in tempo and Clint then took hold of Zack's cock and frantically stroked it. I knew that they were nearing their climax, so I increased my stroking of Brad, hoping to bring him closer to coming with me. He understood and reciprocated with me and then we heard Zack shout out.

"I'm coming, Clint," and a spurt of cum erupted from his cock tip and landed on the ruin's floor, swiftly followed a few more rapid ejaculations.

Clint felt the tightening of Zack's ass muscles on his cock and thrust long and deep and then erupted, filling Zack with warm cum. The two men's bodies shuddered as they released their load and continued to do so until they were emptied of their juices, and at the same time, Brad and I did likewise.

Brad and I looked at each other and kissed gently as a form of saying thanks, while Zack and Clint's mouth clamped together and their arms once again encircled each other. When they felt that they had returned to a sense of tranquility, Zack and Clint parted, pulled on their shorts and left the ancient room, only to see Brad and me also pulling our shorts up.

"Apollo was right," said Zack as he finished pulling up his shorts and tucking his cock into them. "You have a massive cock and know how to use it well."

"Thank you Zack and you have an awesome ass, tight and snug," responded Clint. "But tell me, has Apollo always liked to dominate, if you know what I mean?"

"Do you mean is he like a master?"

"Yes."

"When we were small, he always liked to dominate me, and even as we grew up he carried on like that."

"Zack, may I ask you something personal?"

"Sure, what is it?"

"You and Apollo…?"

Zack laughed.

"You mean have we been together?"

Clint nodded.

Still laughing, Zack replied. "Many times, Clint, and although we have taken turns, he still likes to dominate me."

"And do you like being dominated?"

"Sometimes, but it depends who is my master."

"I liked Apollo," continued Clint and I liked it when he fucked me. In fact he was the first man ever to do that to me."

"You surprise me that you let him dominate you."

"I wanted it and I enjoyed it," said Clint, "but I hope that one day I will return to Greece and that both you and he are together with me; that I would enjoy."

Brad and I reached Zack and Clint and could see their passion still smoldering.

"Did you two like looking at the ruins?" asked Clint.

"We wouldn't call you and Zack ruins," replied Brad, cheekily.

"What do you mean?" enquired Zack.

"They were watching us, Zack," responded Clint.

"You mean while we were …"

"Oh yes," I replied, with a broad smile, "and we thought you were both so into each other it was passionate to watch."

Fortunately both Zack and Clint saw the funny side of it as we had also enjoyed ourselves while being voyeurs.

"Do you want to look around the ruins now?" asked Zack.

Clint looked at his watch and saw that time had raced ahead of us.

"Zack, I think we must be getting back to the ship or we'll be left here forever."

"I would like that," said Zack, hugging Clint and then Brad and I. "Can I walk you back to your ship to see you off?"

"I'd like that," said Clint, putting his arm around Zack's shoulder and the four of us headed back to the ship. "And may I ask a favor of you?"

"Sure, what?" asked Zack.

"I know I probably won't be back until maybe next year, but could I get yours and Apollo's telephone numbers?"

"Only with pleasure," replied Zack, asking also for a pen and some paper to write them down.

He wrote down their names, phone numbers and addresses and handed the paper and pen back to Clint.

"I gave you all the postal details in case you want to write to us. The other details, you know already," said Zack with a delightful smile on his face.

Once we had boarded, we went onto the upper deck and as the ship started to sail, we waved our goodbyes to Zack, who I think was really sorry to see us go, but I felt sure he would be on the phone to Apollo to tell him of our visit and perhaps even of his encounter with Clint.

As we sailed back to Piraeus, we remained almost silent as we thought of our trip today and the unexpected encounter with Zack.

Eventually Clint broke the silence.

"How's that for fate, hey?"

"You mean meeting up with Apollo's brother?" Brad said.

"Yes, and to think they were twins."

"But were they twins in every way, Clint?" I ventured to ask.

Clint knew precisely what I meant. He grinned at me and nodded.

"In almost every way. They are both big boys in build, height and…"

"…and cock size," interjected Brad.

"There you're right again," said Clint. "However, there is one difference."

"What's that?"

"Joe, Apollo is the domineering one of the two. He likes to have his slaves but I think Zack is the gentler and probably more caring of the two."

"Actually, he does seem a very caring person, although we never really got to talk to him," said Brad, "but with regards to looks and physique, I could be quite happy with either of the two men."

"Oh please, you'd be happy with any man so long as he had a big dick and knew how to use it," remonstrated Clint.

Brad and I both roared with laughter, because it was true with regard to both of us and not merely Brad.

Our ship sailed majestically through the blue waters and soon reached the harbor at Piraeus where we disembarked and flagged down a cab to drive us into the heart of Athens.

We had probably been back at the hotel an hour or two when there was a knock on our room door. Clint chose to answer the knock and there stood Dimitri.

"Come in Dimitri. What are you doing here?"

"I came round earlier and the reception said you had gone out this morning. Where did you go and why didn't you tell me you were going somewhere? I could have taken you."

He genuinely sounded disappointed in us for not informing him.

"Dimitri, we decided at the very last minute to go on the day cruise to Hydra and the other close islands," I said.

"Oh," he replied, now sounding more satisfied that we hadn't let him down. "Did you have a nice trip?"

"Very nice, thanks," answered Brad, "but I think Clint enjoyed it more than us."

Dimitri looked bewildered and looked to Clint for some sort of explanation.

Clint merely smiled but never offered any explanation. However, he did say, "Brad had a good time on the ship when we were traveling to the islands, didn't you Brad?"

It was everyone's turn to look at Brad for an explanation, but nothing was forthcoming. Seeing that Dimitri was not about to get any juicy information out of us, I asked why he'd turned up at our hotel.

"I wondered what you might be doing tonight."

"Well, we're leaving tomorrow so we hadn't thought of anything special and we didn't want to have a late night," I offered, as an impromptu explanation.

I don't know whether Dimitri was hoping for a last night with us clubbing or visiting a sauna, but we'd had a long tiring day and weren't up to partying.

"I think we'll probably just go to the Plaka area and have dinner and then get to bed," suggested Clint.

"I take you to Plaka," said Dimitri, deciding that he was not going to give up on us.

We all looked at each other and realized we weren't going to be able to go out without Dimitri, so we relinquished and agreed that he could take us.

"You shower and dress, and then I pick you up here at 8:00p.m," insisted Dimitri.

And so it was agreed that our last night had been planned for us.

CHAPTER 15

DINNER AND ROMANCE

One doesn't dress up in Greece for dinner, unless it's a formal occasion, mainly because of the intense heat, so the three of us pulled on jeans and T-shirts, although we probably would have preferred to wear shorts. After dressing, we made our way downstairs to wait for Dimitri in the lobby of the hotel. I don't know what the staff of the hotel thought of us as whenever they saw us, Dimitri was with us. We didn't have long to wait and soon, our driver and escort arrived.

However, he didn't arrive alone. When we reached his car, there sat Dimitri's date from the night we went out with him to the bar and he'd met this young man upstairs in the cruising area. The three of us squashed ourselves into the back seat of the car.

"Hi", we all chorused together as we entered the car.

The young man smiled back at us and greeted us.

"I am Ari," said the young man.

"Is that short for Aristotle?" enquired Brad, trying to be charming to the young man.

"Yes," he beamed, "But I don't have the brains of the original Aristotle."

We all laughed at his joke, and Dimitri climbed in behind the wheel, started his car and of we went to the Plaka area.

"What do you do?" I asked Ari.

"I'm at university," he answered. "I'm a student there."

"That's great. What are you studying?" I continued.

"Science."

"Well that takes brains," replied Brad, who sounded impressed by Ari's abilities.

"But I don't know what to do when I finish my studies."

"I'm sure you'll have no problem in finding a job if you've graduated with a science degree," I noted.

"We'll have to wait and see."

At first I wondered what a taxi driver saw in a clever young student, but then the more I looked at Ari, the more I realized that Dimitri's attraction for the young man was purely physical and that they probably had nothing in common mentally. Yes, Ari had a pleasant smile and dark, captivating eyes and I remembered noticing in the bar that night, that he also had a cute ass. No doubt, it was Ari's ass that Dimitri craved and maybe Ari was happy to have Dimitri's cock spreading his ass for him.

We seemed to be winding in and out of narrow streets as though we were searching for something. Eventually, Dimitri brought his car to a sudden halt.

"Where are we?" asked Clint, looking around him.

"We are here," said Dimitri, proudly.

He switched off the engine and we all fell out of the car into the heat of the evening; well at least those who were crammed in the back of the car. When we got out, we noticed quite a number of people heading into a simple looking building that really attracted very little attention. We followed the crowds of people into the building and were pleasantly surprised to find a lively restaurant with vibrant music and incessant chatter from the patrons.

Dimitri obviously knew either the matter d' or the owner, because we were speedily escorted to a table and a waiter appeared post haste.

"Do you have friends in high places" asked Clint, "with such prompt service?"

Dimitri felt proud and laughed.

"The owner is a friend of mine," replied Dimitri.

We wondered if the owner knew anything about Dimitri's affection for young men, seeing that Ari was accompanying him and not his wife.

"Tell me, Dimitri," asked Brad in a sotto voce tone, without the others at nearby tables hearing. "What is the situation with Greek men and their wives or girlfriends?"

"What do you mean?" asked Dimitri.

"Well, whenever we go out at night all you see are streets full of men and very few women."

"Women mustn't walk the streets alone," replied Dimitri, "unless of course they are... you know what..."

"You mean prostitutes," I answered.

"Yes," he replied. "So the men go out together and if you have a girlfriend she must accompany you if you want her to, otherwise she must stay at home with the other women."

"No wonder the Greek men like other men," muttered Brad to me.

"So is this why no one questions you being out with Ari?" I asked.

"Exactly!" beamed Dimitri, as the waiter came to take our drinks order. "What would you like to drink, guys?"

"Ouzo for me please," I said.

Both Brad and Clint also decided to indulge in the Greek pleasures while Ari wanted a beer and Dimitri ordered himself a bottle of wine – retsina!

"I don't know how you can drink that stuff," said Clint, screwing up his nose at the thought.

"It is delicious," replied Dimitri, smacking his lips in anticipation of the bottle to come.

The waiter left to collect our drinks and in his place was a blast of loud Greek bouzouki music. The beat was infectious and soon we were all tapping our feet in time to the music and a couple of patrons even got up onto the floor and started dancing to the music.

"You like?" asked Dimitri.

"Yes," replied Brad, "it's very catchy music."

The waiter returned with our drinks and at the same time we placed our orders.

"I'd like souvlakia," said Clint.

"And for me, some moussaka, please," requested Brad.

Not to be outdone, and having picked up some of the Greek language, I asked for "arni lemonato me patates."

Dimitri and Ari burst out laughing at my Greek accent.

"What on earth did you order, Joe?" enquired Clint.

"Just a simple dish of roast garlic lamb with lemon potatoes," I replied, smugly.

"So you not only pick up the language, but you also pick up the Greek boys, hey?" commented Clint, with a touch of sarcasm in his voice.

"Well you didn't do too badly yourself, with Apollo and Zack," I retaliated.

The meals eventually arrived and there was silence from the five of us as we tucked into our various dishes. The only sounds were that of the constant bouzouki sounds and the odd chatter from other patrons.

After our main courses were finished, Dimitri suggested that we all have baklava for dessert, which we did and it was really tasty. After a couple more ouzos and beers for Ari, Dimitri suggested we go to a club to dance the night away.

"Just remember we're leaving tomorrow," I whispered to Clint.

"He's just trying to be nice to us seeing that' it's our last night," he responded.

I couldn't argue with Clint's point of view, but I also knew we had a flight to catch.

"We can always sleep on the plane," said Clint trying to calm me down.

And so it was decided that we'd go to a club for a while before Dimitri would take us back to the hotel.

We once more squeezed into Dimitri's car and headed around the windy streets of the Plaka area in search of the club he wanted to visit. We eventually arrived there and alighted.

The club was pretty dark and dingy, from what could be seen, so perhaps it was a good thing that it was so dark inside, we wouldn't have to worry what was around us.

"What the eye can't see, the heart won't worry about," said the philosophical Brad as we entered the dark club.

One just had to follow the sound of the thumping music to know where to go, and that's precisely what we did. Again, Dimitri took charge of the evening and ordered drinks for us, based on what we'd been drinking in the restaurant, and then he and Ari disappeared onto the dance floor. The music in the club was not typically Greek in nature and was more Western commercial.

"Come Clint, do you wanna dance?" asked Brad.

The two of them headed onto the dance floor to join Dimitri and Ari in the semi-dark.

"You dance?" said a deep voice behind me.

I turned around and in the smallest amount of light available, I saw a large man standing with an outstretched hand to me. I couldn't make out in the limited light what his facial features were like, but decided that I had nothing to lose by having a dance with him, so we too went onto the semi-dark dance floor.

I felt a little better when I saw Clint and Brad there and moved closer to them.

"Who's your friend?" asked Brad, when I neared him.

"Don't know," I replied.

"Doesn't look too bad," resumed Brad.

"If you say so. I couldn't see him properly in the darkness."

We carried on dancing until the music ended and then my partner asked if I wanted a drink.

"No thanks, I still have one."

"You need toilet?" he asked.

I thought this a rather odd question to ask and replied that I didn't need the toilet.

He ignored my answer.

"I take you there," he said, as though deaf to my response.

Taking me by the hand he led me down a long, narrow corridor, down a flight of stairs and into a smelly toilet. The lighting in the toilet seemed far better than that in the club. At the urinal stood a tall, dark man who seemed not to be doing anything. My dance partner walked up to the communal urinal, unzipped and pulled out a long, thick uncut cock and started stroking it to get it hard. I stood and watched, but so did the dark man already standing there, look.

My partner's cock became harder and grew in girth and length and I watched as the dark man crept closer to my dance partner, still staring at the growing muscle that my partner was playing with. As soon as the dark man got next to my partner, the dance partner turned to me and said, "Come here and take this."

He was offering me his cock but I was a little anxious with the dark man still standing there. My dance partner waved his hardened shaft at me showing how well he was endowed. His foreskin had by now peeled right back to reveal a shiny smooth cock head.

Before I had a chance to take a step closer, the dark man had sunk to his knees and engulfed my partner's cock in his mouth.

"Aargh, yes!" growled my partner as the dark man's mouth slobbered along the thick shaft.

I stood watching with fascination and getting harder myself. I let my hand drift over my hardening crotch and felt my own shaft thicken. I didn't have to stand for very long, because suddenly my dance partner let out a loud groan and thrust his crotch deeply into the dark man's face, obviously firing his load down the man's throat. I stood and watched until my partner was empties of all his cum, had zipped up and left to go upstairs. I didn't move. I don't know why I didn't, but I had found the whole episode bewildering, until the dark man rose to his feet and turned to me, his slick cock in his hand. I immediately turned and headed in the same direction my dance partner had gone – back to the dance floor.

"Where have you been?" asked Clint, when he saw me.

"You don't want to know," I replied, still bewildered.

"Are you okay?"

"I think so Clint. I've just been watching the weirdest thing. A dark guy was giving my dance partner a blow-job in the toilet."

"And you weren't involved?"

"No."

"Hell, you're losing your touch," said Clint as a jibe. "So is it busy there?"

"No. There were only us two and the dark guy."

"So where's your dance partner now?"

"Haven't a clue, but I left the dark guy down there, so I presume he's waiting for the next person to go into the toilet."

"Is he worth visiting?" asked Clint, and I screwed up my nose.

"I'm not sure if you can see my reaction in this light, but I think you'd have better taste, so don't waste your time going there, unless you really want to have a piss."

"Okay, I'll take your word for it," replied Clint, letting go of the subject.

"What are you two so ensconced in conversation about?" asked Brad, now joining us.

"I was just offering Clint a date with a strange, dark man."

"You offer him a date and not me? So that's what you call friendship?" remarked a bitter Brad.

"Go to the toilet and see how fast you'll be back," I suggested, but Brad got the message and refrained from rushing off to the toilet.

Dimitri and Ari had seemed to have disappeared and I knew that they weren't down in the toilet or I would have seen them.

"Where's our horny driver?" I asked, generally.

No one seemed to know, but we weren't unduly worried.

Three-quarters of an hour later, Ari and Dimitri returned from wherever they'd been and both had broad smiles and seemed to be floating on air.

"You two seem to have a light step about you," remarked Brad.

"I don't know what you mean?" asked Ari.

"You seem to be very happy, is what I mean," said Brad, winking knowingly to Ari.

"Oh!" giggled Ari. "You know what Dimitri is like."

I certainly knew what Dimitri was like from the first day we arrived in Athens.

"Did you enjoy it," I asked surreptitiously.

Ari grinned broadly and nodded his head enthusiastically.

The night went by very quickly and before we knew it, it was time to head back to the hotel for a few hours' sleep and then off to the airport. Dimitri dropped us at our hotel where we said goodbye to Ari, not knowing if we'd see him later in the morning when Dimitri came to take us to the airport, and headed off to bed.

CHAPTER 16

THE HOME JOURNEY

The following morning we awoke to yet another hot Athenian day, similar to what we'd experienced during our holiday. We rose and showered, and then dressed in casual traveling clothes for the journey home, and then booked out of our hotel and headed off to the airport to catch our flight home.

Dimitri had promised to take us to the airport, but when he arrived at the hotel, we noticed that he didn't have his friend, Ari, with him. We asked him why he hadn't brought his friend from two nights before and he just smiled and said, "No room in the car."

We thought this somewhat strange as we'd all been in the car the night before, but we decided that it was better not to elaborate on the topic, and rather let things slide. Maybe it was fine to go out with another guy during the evening, but it might be looked down upon to do so during the day when anyone could see you with the other person. We did, however, notice that the whole way to the airport, Dimitri seemed to have this fixed contented smile across his face. Obviously he was very happy with his evening's performance with Ari! I often wondered if his wife had any idea as to what he might be up to with Ari and other boys like him, but that was none of my business.

Once we arrived at the airport, we booked in our luggage and said our farewells to Dimitri and thanked him for all his kindness while we had been in Athens.

"Thank you so much for everything, Dimitri," I said, hugging him closely to me.

"You are welcome, Joe," he replied, with a tinge of sadness in his voice. "It is always sad to make friends and then see them go."

"I'm sure that we'll be back," said Clint, also hugging Dimitri and going so far as to kiss him on both cheeks.

"That I'm also sure of," echoed Brad, "if not to stay in Athens, definitely to go to Mykonos."

We all knew the real reason why Brad wanted to go back to Mykonos, but he said it was because of the crystal clear sea water and the friendly people on the island.

"I will miss you guys," said Dimitri, looking like a sad puppy. "It was so much fun to take you around Athens and to share my city with you."

"Well, we'll always remember you and what you did for us," I said, hugging him again.

I could sense that he didn't want us to go and would have been quite happy to keep us in Athens, maybe even just to do things for us. I wondered if perhaps we'd brought something out of Dimitri that might have been dormant in him for a long time. I also wondered if he'd done things with us that he might have desired to do in the past, but never had the right company to do it with. Whatever it was, I knew that Dimitri had become another person thanks to us meeting him.

I also knew that Brad, Clint and I had also become different people. Things had happened to us during our holiday that had changed our attitudes and outlook on life, in most cases, for the good. Let's not forget Clint losing his virginity! That in itself was an accomplishment.

After many more hugs and kisses on the cheeks, we watched Dimitri drive off, and then we went through to the departure lounge and waited to board our plane.

We sat and each of us quietly thought about our holiday, the events that impacted on us directly as a group and those things that impacted on us individually. I knew that my relationship with Brad and Clint had been more securely cemented and that we had been drawn inexplicably closer to each other. We were deep in thought when our concentration was disrupted by an announcement that we were about to board our plane.

We queued up with the other passengers and slowly made our way on board. It was a pleasure to get into the coolness of the plane, away from the steaming heat outside. We found our seats, three next to each other, and settled in to make ourselves comfortable. Once all the passengers were on board, the doors were closed, the engines started and we taxied down the runway and set off for home, leaving behind the glorious Greek islands and the majestically blue sea. Drinks were brought around and we settled ourselves in for a long flight back home.

The first thing that Brad did was to survey the Greek stewards on the plane to see if there were any who might be eligible to 'entertain' him during the flight.

"Haven't you had enough sex for a while, Brad?" asked Clint as he watched his friend eyeing each steward that walked past our row of seats.

"I can't even spell the word enough," replied the cheeky Brad, with an impish grin across his face.

"Did you enjoy your holiday?" I asked, turning to Clint.

"Absolutely!" came the reply. "Thanks for suggesting that we come to Greece. I must admit that I had my doubts, but once we got here and the fun started, I'll be honest, I'm sad to be going home," he continued.

"You see, I told you that you would have a good time here and that the Greeks were phenomenal people."

"Phenomenal isn't the word," said Brad, "Stunning and sexy are more like it."

Just then one of the flight stewards came walking down the aisle. Brad nudged me as he saw him.

"I see what you mean," I said smiling at the air steward.

He stopped when he reached our seats.

"Is there anything I can get for you gentlemen?" he asked.

Brad and I looked at each other and winked.

"Well actually we were just wondering…" said Brad.

Clint immediately cut in. "I don't think my friends really want anything, but thanks for offering."

The steward looked a little surprised at first, until Brad intervened.

"How dare you," came Brad's retort to Clint. "We were just wondering what was for dinner."

"The menu will be brought to you soon, sir," answered the polite steward and left for the galley.

"A likely story," sighed Clint. "You were probably going to ask him if he was available."

"I would never do such a thing," laughed Brad.

"Well, at least you tried," I said giving Brad a squeeze on his leg. "Wait until Clint's asleep, then we'll try the steward again."

"Don't you even think about it," came Clint's threat. "I have every intention of staying awake to keep an eye on you two."

The menus were brought around the plane and then dinner was served with more drinks after which we settled down to watch the film being shown. Each passenger had been given a blanket so we threw our blankets over ourselves and snuggled in to watch the film.

I didn't find the film interesting, so I channel hopped on the television in order to find something worthwhile to watch. I also noted that Brad was doing likewise, until he got tired of looking for something that interested him, and turned his attention back to the steward he had seen earlier.

"You're not getting ideas, are you Brad?" I asked.

He turned to me and shrugged.

"Well at least he's better to look at than the movies we've got to choose from."

"You really are a glutton for punishment," I joked.

After some time, Clint, who'd become bored with watching the movie, said that he was going to sleep, and Brad and I concurred that we would join him. We closed our eyes and snuggled up closer to each other, well as close as one can get with armrests in the way, and went to sleep.

I can't really sleep sitting upright in a plane, so I spent most of the flight tossing and turning in my seat. So did Brad, for that matter, but Clint seemed to be dead to the world and having sweet dreams. Brad, who was sitting between Clint and me, nudged at one point during the flight and whispered, "Give me your hand."

I gave him my right hand and felt as he pulled my arm past him and over towards Clint. "Feel this," he said, gently laying my hand on Clint's cock, which was standing erect.

"Do you think he's dreaming of Apollo?" I asked.

"Well he's had so many on this holiday, who knows," came Brad's whispered reply.

"I'll lay my bets that it's Apollo who he's dreaming about. Should I squeeze it?" I asked.

"No, he might wake up," came Brad's reply.

"He is awake!" came a dry reply from Clint, "and it was Apollo that I had been dreaming about, but you two had also been in the dream, and so don't feel left out."

"Tell me Clint, in the dream were you fucking Apollo or vice versa?" whispered Brad.

"He was fucking me," came Clint's whispered reply.

"I knew he was a slave to Apollo," I said.

"Come to think of it, so were you and Brad."

Of course, Clint was right, but I had said that earlier after our episode with Apollo, however, I don't think they realized just how much we had become infatuated by this man.

"Where does this put us?" I asked.

"Meaning?" enquired Brad.

"Well apart from him drugging you, for which you really had no control, we all fell under his spell as though we'd been drugged.

We also wanted to be dominated by him; well all except Clint, initially."

"I'm glad you finished the sentence, Joe. When he had treated Brad badly, I wanted to kill the guy I was so cross, but then I got to see another side of him and it was weird," replied Clint.

"Weird in what way?" asked Brad.

"Well, I have never been screwed, sexually speaking, by anyone in my life, yet I allowed him to do it to me. In fact there was something about him that was attracting me to him, or perhaps him to me, because I really wanted him to fuck me and I can't explain why."

"Maybe it was his big dick," I volunteered.

"No," said Clint, "Because he's not as big as me so it wasn't that. Perhaps it was just the idea of someone else dominating me for once. You know, just to see what it felt like."

"I personally think each of us has our own reason for being attracted to Apollo and him to us, but I agree with you about the feeling of being dominated, especially by someone bigger or stronger than you," I observed.

"I don't know about you guys, but all this talk of sex and sexy men is turning me on," said Brad, adjusting the erection in his jeans which he had acquired. "I think I'm going to take a walk."

"Well you can't walk very far," came a snide remark from Clint.

"You're right, just as far as the back of the plane where the crew is usually situated," replied Brad, standing up and getting out of his seat. "I'll see you guys in the morning."

With that, Brad left his seat and Clint snuggled down to go to sleep, while I tried to see if Brad had made contact with his Greek steward. I failed to see them so I also covered myself with my blanket, closed my eyes and tried to go to sleep.

It was in the early hours of the morning that I awoke with Brad accidentally bumping my leg as he returned to his seat.

"Busy night, buddy?" I asked.

He covered himself with his blanket and I felt a hand come wandering under my blanket and land on my crotch. Brad's hand lay there for the rest of the duration of the flight, gently squeezing my cock every so often until I had a hard-on, then he was happy.

"Sorry Joe," he whispered, "It's just that I've felt something hard all night and I can't get to sleep unless I've got something hard in my hand!"

Likely story, I thought!

The rest of the flight remained uneventful, and finally in the early hours of the next morning, we were served breakfast and then prepared for our arrival back home.

As the wheels of the plane touched down, a feeling of happiness overcame me; I was glad to be in our own country, but ready to start planning our next holiday to Greece.

"Do you think that the next time we go to Greece we should go to a different island?" I asked, more out of fun, but a chorus greeted me from Clint and Brad, "NO!"

"OK," I said, "I'm happy with your decision, but I don't think we need to go to Delos again, after all, we've seen everything there is to see there!"

I thought Clint and Brad were going to kill me when I said that, but I just laughed and said, "I'm joking; I'm not serious," before the blows and punches rained down on me.

Ever since our return, we've not stopped talking about Apollo and our experiences but Clint's attitude has changed; he's not so moody anymore, and he's very keen to visit Greece again, but he still won't let either Brad or I get to screw him – poor man, he doesn't know what he's missing!

THE END

ABOUT THE AUTHOR

Lew Bull

LEW BULL has now had 10 books published by Nazca Plains. This novel adds to his collection of novels titled, *Power Buddies*; *Wet, Wild & Willing*; *The Bonds of Friendship*; *Caribbean Cruising*; *Memoirs of a Hustler*; *Shadows* and *Rough Cut*. Added to these are his two anthologies, one of exotic cocktail recipes accompanied by equally erotic stories entitled, *Cocktales* and the other, *Mystique*. His novel *Wet, Wild & Willing* was nominated for the 2008 National Leather Association (International) writing award. Other recent anthologies that contain his work include, *Cruise Lines*; *Taken By Force*; *Boys Will Be Boys*; *Don't Ask, Don't Tie Me Up - Military BDSM Fantasies*; *Service with a Smile*; *Pretty Boys & Roughnecks*; *Special Forces and Sex Time-Travel*. He is involved in education and lives in Johannesburg, South Africa where he enjoys spending time with his partner of thirty-four years and traveling as often as he can.

tales

by

Lew Bull

MEMOIRS OF A
HUSTLER

A NOVEL BY
LEW BULL

MYSTIQUE

LEW
BULL

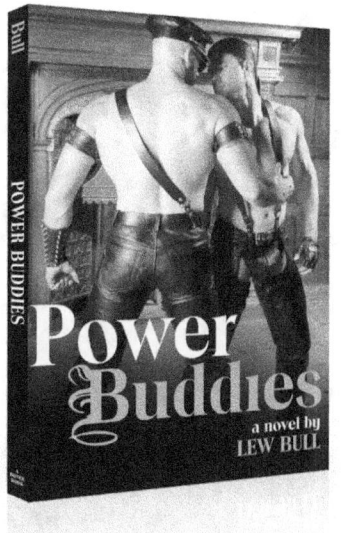

Power
Buddies

a novel by
LEW BULL

www.ingramcontent.com/pod-product-compliance
Lightning Source LLC
Chambersburg PA
CBHW050658290626
47170CB00015B/1678